I0545880

FIND ME

∞ ∞

GRACE BRANNIGAN

P.O. Box 100
East Jewett, New York, 12424 USA

Find Me
Women of Character Contemporary Series
Echoes From the Past
Once and Always
Heartstealer
Wishing on a Rodeo Moon

Women of Strength Time Travel Series
Once Upon a Remembrance
Soulmates Through Time
Treasure So Rare

Romantic Short Stories
Two Babies, a Cowboy and Sara
Deception

Faeries Lost Series
Find Me
Whisper Me
Hear Me

Website: www.GraceBrannigan.com

All Characters, places and events are fictitious and are not associated or inspired by any person living or dead.

Cover art by Steph's Cover Design

Print Edition Copyright 2015 Elaine Warfield

ISBN: 978-1-939061-46-1

License Notes

All rights reserved. This book is protected under the copyright laws of the United States of America. No part of this book may be reproduced by any means whatsoever, mechanical, photographic, electronic or in the form of an audio recording or stored in a retrieval system, transmitted or otherwise be copied for public or private use—other than for brief quotations in articles and reviews without prior written consent from the publisher Questor Books.

Thank you for respecting the hard work of this author. Happy reading!

∞ Chapter One ∞

The naked woman lay on the road thirty feet ahead of Drew Maddox's truck. He hit the brakes, then fought desperately for control as his tires kept turning in the fresh snow. He turned the wheel and his truck slid precariously close to a flimsy guard rail, the only thing between him and a sixty-foot drop. When the truck finally shuddered to a stop, his headlights were a beam in the night, hitting the steel bridge just ahead. He'd never expected to see anything in the road this far out of town, certainly not a woman.

Thin strings of blue light snapped like electricity in the night sky, sparks showering down like a pyrotechnic display.

His truck rattled ominously, then went dead, killing the headlights. He shoved open the door and a scream cut through him like a dull filet knife. The eerie quiet that followed settled a shiver across his shoulders.

Grimly, Drew grabbed a flashlight and exited the vehicle. The woman lay with one arm propping her up, head down, deep red hair hanging to the pavement. Blood stained her neck and temple and her skin appeared wet. Her lower body appeared bound by strips of dark fabric from her hips to her feet.

Keeping the light on her, he ran toward her as she lifted her head. He stopped. Her eyes reflected the light like a cat's eyes, gold reflecting back at him. His years in law enforcement had made him pretty much shockproof, but now he dropped the light.

Scrambling furiously, he retrieved the flashlight and shone it back over the area.

She was gone.

The only thing left behind was the black binding and a scorch mark easily six feet in diameter.

Drew hurried to where he'd seen the woman. The scorched area was bone dry while the rest of the road was covered by several inches of snow. Inside the scorched area lay black strips of material, which had already begun to disintegrate.

He touched the dry pavement, but quickly pulled back as residual sparks jumped along the surface. "What the -- Don't tell me aliens," he muttered. Where was the woman?

Hearing something behind him he turned quickly, but saw nothing except shadows beyond the guard rail. "Anybody there?" He ran his flashlight up and down the road.

The air had a weird pulse, pushing at him, and he ducked his head as snow pelted him. When it finally abated, he lifted his head and blinked hard. The woman was lying in the road again.

Stuff like this didn't happen.

The electrical sparks seemed to have dissipated, so he quickly moved into the scorched circle to kneel beside her, the pavement warm even though the air was frigid. Snow swirled viciously around them. "Hey, can you hear me? We have to get you out of here. Can you get up?"

She lay unresponsive, eyes closed, her skin almost as white as the snow.

"Good God, you're going to freeze to death." Drew shrugged out of his jacket, lifting her shoulders to place it under her and buttoning her into it. Her flesh felt like ice. He kept an arm around her as she sagged against him. In stark contrast to her pale skin, scarlet seeped from horrific burn marks at her temple and right shoulder. In a quick assessment, he took note of a possibly infected tattoo on her arm. At least she appeared to be breathing. The burn marks at her temple distorted her cheek and jaw, the skin swollen and fiery red. It looked really bad and he worried about injuring her further in moving her, but she'd die out here, there was no choice.

He hit speed dial on his cell and waited to be connected to 911.

No cell service.

Swearing under his breath -- she wasn't very big but she was all dead weight -- Drew managed to lift her into his arms, carrying her with her left side against him. A thick, twisted braid of red hair swung against his neck as he carried her. The jacket was the only thing protecting her, and he sure knew it wasn't going to be enough. An intense pulsing energy throbbed where her body touched his, but otherwise she felt wet and intensely cold.

"Drew."

He didn't think anything could shock him anymore, but hearing his name on this woman's lips did, and the fact that her voice struck a familiar chord.

"I'm going to get you help," he said, his thoughts racing. Who was she? Why did something about her seem familiar?

Wasting no time, he managed to get the passenger door to his truck open and lay her on the cloth seat. Running around to the driver's side, he yanked the door open and jumped inside, hoping it would start. He turned the key and got lucky as the engine turned over.

Cranking up the heater, he reached behind his seat and pulled out an emergency thermal blanket. Carefully, he maneuvered her onto her side with her bare feet against the passenger door. That's when he saw by the interior light hundreds of tiny, oozing blood spots from her hips down to her feet. The burn marks on her right side were horrific. Adrenalin racing, not sure what he'd stumbled into, Drew feared time was not on her side. He tucked the thermal blanket around her and reversed his truck. A bright flash of light behind him, almost like an explosion, had him hitting the brakes. He put out a hand to keep the woman from falling off the seat, then drove forward to get away from the billowing smoke.

Once clear, he again reversed the truck, glancing repeatedly in his rear view mirror to see if anyone was following him.

Tonight it was one freakish occurrence on top of another. He glanced at her in the dim light and took in a full bottom lip, the curve of her left, unmarred cheek, almost-black lashes in contrast to her bright red hair. She was somewhere in her twenties. As a private investigator he never forgot a face and something about her pulled at strings of memory. He'd remember in time.

Cynically, Drew hoped the past wasn't coming back to bite him. There'd been a time about a year after Deborah's death that he'd gone on a bender, dating pretty much all the eligible females he came into contact with. He wasn't particularly proud of that time in his life, but ultimately he'd come to realize he needed to focus on work instead of jumping into a new relationship. His ex, with her clinging dependence, had at least taught him that. These days, work seemed an easier solution than a personal life.

Her eyes. What had eyes like that except for cats and other animals? His glance fell to her face again. Annoyed at himself, he looked back to the road. Trying to figure out her identity would have to wait until she woke up. If she woke up.

Meanwhile, the road was snowy and dangerous; he'd better pay attention and not land them in a ditch. He'd get her to the hospital and then get back to his business. He was in the middle of an important investigation and he'd been on his way out to meet with his client Mary Palmer when all this happened.

Mary was gravely ill and all she wanted was for him to find her husband Rick. The job had a short timeline but promised a big payout. Drew needed that money to finally settle Deborah's bills and then he'd have that stress off his back forever. Mary had photographs waiting for him and then he could get going on the case. Mary was a sweet old lady struggling with each breath, an around the clock nurse, and her old man was missing in action. Not his normal investigative case, but the money was right so who was he to quibble over the details?

"What the --" Drew hit the brakes again as he swerved away from a man standing in the road. Luckily he hadn't been going fast. He turned in his seat to look behind him but didn't see anything or anyone. This was playing too much like déjà vu out here.

He had the weirdest notion the guy had vanished just before he would have hit him. The whole thing left him feeling pretty uneasy.

He checked the woman. She'd worked one of her arms out of the thermal blanket. The arm with the tattoo. He stared at it, perplexed. It was no longer swollen, but there was something different ... he counted the points. Eleven. He was good with details. There had been fewer points on the tattoo when he'd seen it earlier. This was getting freakier by the moment. Tattoos don't change on their own.

Her breath was so shallow it almost seemed as if she weren't breathing at all, but she did move her head.

"Are you awake? I'm taking you to the hospital,"

he said, tucking her arm back under the blanket. "I'm Drew Maddox. I found you on the road out by Dell's Bridge. You're pretty badly injured," he added, then began to drive once more, peering with difficulty through the blowing snow.

"No." Her voice came out a dry croak.

Drew glanced away from the road a moment. He could just make out the gleam of her eyes, now looking normal, in the gleam of the dashboard lights. "A hospital is the place you need to be. You're in rough shape."

"Take me back." She struggled to sit upright. "Back to where you found me." Her voice came out a thin thread.

"There's nothing out there," he said patiently. "We're in the middle of a blizzard. You'll die."

She shook her head.

"What's your name?" he asked.

She put her head back against the truck seat, her blue eyes having an unsettling intensity. "Pandimora."

"Pandimora." Drew shook his head. "I get the feeling I know you."

The wind hit the truck with unbelievable force, shaking it.

"He's coming for me."

"Who? The person who did this?" He turned on one of the small overhead lights. Perplexed, Drew looked at her head and shoulder where he'd seen raw burn marks only ten minutes ago, but now there were only patches of red, as if she'd healed. "Those were pretty serious burns --" he stared at her suspiciously, slowing the truck and pulling to the side of the road. "What is this -- some kind of game? Real burns don't heal like that," he said.

"This is not a game," she said. "I was burned."

"Tell me what's going on," he said harshly. "I don't like being taken for a fool."

He gripped the shifting lever to put the truck in drive, but she grabbed his wrist with surprising strength. He couldn't remove his hand. He stared down at wispy blue sparks snapping where she'd grabbed his wrist. His skin tingled.

"Who are you?" he ground out.

She released him and he was able to let go of the shifting lever. The blue sparks dissipated.

"How did you do that?"

Drew stared at her, then avoided her eyes. Looking into their clear blue depths, he had a disorienting sensation of falling. He blinked hard several times. "I've seen you before," he said. "I get a feeling I should know you, but the memory's just not there."

"It doesn't matter now," she said. "I need to go back." She sat up and looked out the back window. "If I stay, he'll find me."

"Who?"

"The elder."

"You'd have died in the cold." He stared at her searchingly. "Is this gang related? Or is it an abusive boyfriend?"

"You might find the truth difficult."

He gave her a cynical smile. "Trust me, I've heard all the stories."

"An Aisywel elder tried to kill me." He noted the faint tremor of her shoulders. Drew, who had a high freak out threshold, got a chill up his neck.

"What is Aisywel?" he asked.

She spoke slowly, as if testing his reaction. "Aisywel is where the faeries live. Aisywel is -- was -- my home."

Drew leaned back. Geez. He hadn't seen that one coming. "You're a faerie?" He rubbed his forehead, wondering if she was suffering from delusions. "Did you hit your head? I've got to get you to a hospital."

"No. No. No!"

"Calm down," he said as her agitation increased. For a split second he thought of Deborah. She'd do crazy things when she didn't get her way, like jump out of a moving vehicle or grab the wheel while he was driving down the interstate. She never thought ahead to the consequences of her actions.

"I said you may find the truth difficult," she said flatly, shrugging. The thermal blanket slid down her shoulder. Drew pulled it back up.

"You have to admit that's an unusual -- what kind of place is this Aisywel?" He'd humor her. Maybe she was trying to tell him something important in a round-about way.

"Aisywel is a place of great joy and light," she said quietly, proudly, then added hesitantly, "At least it always has been."

"And someone from this place of great joy tried to kill you?" he asked skeptically. "Kind of contrary, don't you think?"

"But it's true. I managed to escape. Now please take me back. I'm too weak to get there myself."

As he watched she pulled down the thermal blanket, let it pool at her waist. Before his eyes, a blouse and pants slowly appeared and covered her body under his jacket.

Drew jerked back in his seat. "This is a trick. Either you're a magician or I'm dreaming," he muttered.

"There are no tricks involved. Please, please take me back." Drew would swear her pleading was in earnest.

"All right, all right," he said, "but if there's no one out there I'm driving you to town. You'll have to explain to the sheriff what's going on and get checked out at the hospital." She needed some kind of medical attention.

She looked down. "This covering has my scent," she muttered, apparently distracted. She gathered the emergency blanket into a ball in her arms. "I must wipe away all knowledge of my presence here in this dimension. All strings of memory go to the place lost and not yet found," she said, frowning.

"There's a lost and not yet found? Come on, this is too much," Drew said, driving back to Dell's Bridge. "I can't believe I'm driving you back out there."

"The earth realm is the only place with such a dimension," she said seriously. "All things lost remain there until they are found at the appropriate moment. In Aisywel, nothing is lost."

Pandimora, if that was her real name, needed help. At least now she was conscious but he was still worried about her condition. But he didn't need a woman who would harm herself either. He'd get back to Dell's Bridge as quickly as possible and then back to town.

He felt vibrations beneath his truck and slowed to a crawl. "What now?" he muttered, peering ahead. "That felt like a tremor of some kind."

"It's too late. The elder is getting closer!" she cried and put her bare foot over his on the accelerator pedal.

Drew couldn't get his foot free and the truck jumped ahead on the slippery road, the rear end fishtailing. Quickly, he shifted into neutral as the engine revved high. "Stop!" he said. "You're going to kill both of us."

She pressed back against the seat and pulled her foot away.

Angrily, he turned to her. "Listen, you do this my way or I'm not taking you back out there. Keep on your own side of the seat. These conditions are hazardous enough without you getting crazy."

Pressing her lips together, she nodded.

"Have you taken any drugs in the last two hours?"

"No. We are in grave danger from the elder. I'm sorry but I was desperate to get away." Her voice was now low. "Please forgive me."

"Sit still and I'll get us there, but I won't have you messing around or pulling a stunt like that again. Do you understand?"

Biting her lips, she nodded.

∞ Chapter Two ∞

Pandimora shifted on the truck seat, stifling a groan as movement stirred pain like hot flames, licking the inside of her skin. She squeezed her eyes closed, trying to push away the memories as heavy energy rushed at her like smoky residue. Her chest felt tight, uncomfortable. She feared what lurked out there, rushing after her, trying to take her back. As her heart pumped the blood wildly through her, her body told her it was dying. Her conscious mind was aware of the internal breakdown of her body and she had to force herself to remain upright in the seat.

Drew's shoulder and arm next to her felt solid. She had never been so intimately close to a human before. She had seen Drew from a distance his entire life, but after their childhood, they had never spoken, never touched. She could feel the anger emanating from him. Her shoulders slumped. It had not been the right thing to do, to try to get him to go faster. She felt foolish, but fear had overtaken her, so now she sat tensely, trying to slow her breathing and the panic winding through her.

Even in her fear, her faerie senses remained sharp. She heard the steady, strangely reassuring beat of his heart, felt the blood coursing strongly through his veins. As they continued down the road, she looked back. Surely even the elder would be slowed down by the earth's density and this storm. That was in their favor.

"We won't get far if we can't hide," she muttered, but knew she was too weak to create even a temporary masking dimension to hide them.

"I don't see anyone behind us," Drew said, glancing at her, then back at the road.

Pandimora feared Lukais could find them no matter how fast they drove. Despair settled on her shoulders and she began to shake. Had she escaped his wrath only to die on the earth dimension? And what about Drew? She had also endangered him!

"I'll do my best to protect you," she said now.

He looked at her, one dark blond eyebrow raised. Distracted, Pandimora studied the attractive face next to her, the square jaw, deep set brown eyes. Something inside her chest fluttered.

"Level with me," he said, his voice no nonsense. "Tell me what's really going on."

Pandimora stared at Drew, biting her lip. He might well die for his efforts. He had no understanding what he was up against.

"It's faerie magic." She felt nauseous, even though her stomach was empty. Her entire body ached as the insidious poison seeped into every cell. Lukais had poisoned her. The black poison from beneath the earth's dimension. She gritted her teeth.

Faeries did not normally feel the cold in the earth realm, but now she felt chilled down to her faerie bones. She wanted to close her eyes, but feared she could lapse into an everlasting coma and her immortality would slowly and surely be sapped away.

"I swear your eyes looked like cat eyes when I shined the flashlight earlier. How did you do that?"

"I am a faerie." She shrugged at the disbelief emanating from him.

"Can you see in the dark?"

She nodded, trying to keep her head upright. She had the urge to curl into a ball.

"When I first saw your burns you looked at death's door, but now the burns appear to have healed. Either it's a good makeup job or you heal faster than anyone I've ever seen. Are you really sick?"

Pandimora felt tired, wishing he had not been dragged into this. "I was poisoned. I am not okay." Faeries didn't lie.

"How did you get poisoned?"

"His dark tentacles wrapped around me."

"Those black strips," he muttered.

"Where I entered your dimension lies a healing sanctuary. Right now it's my only hope." Pandimora felt the raw heat emanating from his body. "The elder is more powerful than anything your world knows," she said abruptly.

"Do we have any chance of making it to Dell's Bridge?"

"I'm not sure." She hesitated. "Lukais may stop at nothing to silence me."

"What did you do to piss him off?"

"I eavesdropped on a private conversation." She swallowed. "I heard him making plans to restrict all worlds' access to the universe's natural resources. We have so much in Aisywel and yet he is greedy for more." She shivered when she thought of the full extent of the elder's plans. "He will use the crystal power to create even more havoc in the earth's atmosphere, with destructive, irreversible results. It will affect the food supply of nations already starving. How can I hear this and allow it to happen? The faerie he struck down disagreed with him and was equally horrified."

"That's a pretty incredible story," Drew said. "It almost sounds like a science fiction movie."

"It's the truth." She wasn't sure if he believed her.

"I might be able to erect a temporary barrier to protect us," she said now, hesitantly. "But I would need your help."

"What do you want me to do?" She heard the wariness in his voice. He didn't believe her but she would do her best to protect him.

She chewed her lip. "I've never done this with a human, but my sister and I have many times created a protective barrier when we came to this dimension. I am very weak, but if we share energy, I might be able to create a temporary invisibility. Please stop the vehicle. I don't know how this energy exchange might affect you."

She heard his sigh. "Really?"

She nodded earnestly.

Drew drove the truck to the side of the road and turned to her.

Taking his hands in hers, Pandimora held them firmly, trying to concentrate on igniting a flare of energy between them. Drew's hands were large in comparison to hers, slightly rough and calloused. She opened her eyes, looked down where their hands were joined. A few thin strings of blue light curled around their fingers.

"What is that?" he asked.

She leaned back against the seat, releasing his hands. "It's not enough. I'm too weak."

"When you grabbed my wrist earlier I saw the same blue lights. Is that what you mean? How does that even happen?"

"If I felt well, I would build a bubble of energy around us by using the heat of our skin surfaces. The molecules in the air spaces would vibrate and that would shield us, at least temporarily, from the elder. I thought that perhaps with your strength and vigor, I could compensate my energy for yours and create the same effect." In her agitation she had trouble catching her breath.

"Relax," he said. "Take slow breaths. You only held my palms. What if we connected more skin surface -- would that make a difference?"

Pandimora nodded, trying to calm herself. "It might, and the storm aids us by creating a heavy atmospheric shield of sorts, but we have to hurry. Take my hands again, then slide your palms up to my elbows and I will do the same to you."

After a slight hesitation, Drew did as she instructed, his slightly calloused fingertips moving from her hands to her wrist and then up her arm under the lightweight sleeves of her blouse. A shiver coursed through her, jumping under her skin. Even in her weakness, she was strangely affected by the touch of his fingers against her skin.

Pandimora pushed at his more tightly woven sleeves. "I need you to push your shirt sleeves up so our skin makes direct contact," she said.

Drew leaned forward, pulled his sweatshirt off

and was left with his t-shirt, which clung to his body. Pandimora's mouth went dry. There were no faeries like Drew. His t-shirt outlined a chest hard with muscle, a few tufts of dark blond hair at the top of the shirt. Trolls were the only ones she knew in the world of the fae with hair on their torsos and she'd never found herself attracted in the least to trolls. Was it because she'd watched him from afar, curious about this human?

She looked up and caught his eyes giving her a similar perusal. Her breasts tingled. She shivered in the warm cab, a sensuous heat moving through her. There was no embarrassment. Faeries never experienced such an emotion in relation to themselves. No matter what shape their bodies took, they were a perfect creation.

She needed to focus. "We must hurry," she muttered. "We need to create enough heat for there to be a significant rise in temperature, which will build the energy between us and therefore the shield."

She gripped the muscled contour of his arms as he firmly gripped her arms at the elbow. Pandimora closed her eyes and envisioned the energy building between them, felt her own state of flux, her body system in partial shutdown, then she felt his pulse increase, heard his breathing grow deeper. Suddenly, she felt an increasing warmth. Drew's energy. His life force. It was working. Even from behind her closed lids, she could see that bright strings of light snapped and crackled around them, transforming the inside of the truck to a bright blue halo of light. She held onto him with her limited strength, his energy filling and reviving her to a degree, winding through her as they merged into one. The mingled energy rose to a deep, uplifting crescendo, affecting them down to the cellular level, reaction coursing through nerve endings almost to the point of physical pleasure. With difficulty, she pulled away and gently disengaged contact. Drew jerked back against the seat.

Her flesh wanted to remain close to him; she had actually begun to crave the contact. She felt confused by such a reaction to a human. Pandimora felt the shudder that went through him, saw his jaw clench, and she knew he'd been similarly affected by their contact. She had heard stories of the intensity of sensory circuits when lovemaking occurred between a human and faerie, and this brief experience made her even more curious.

She called upon her boosted energy reserves to erect a temporary veil of protection around them, also incorporating the increasing intensity of the weather into the shield. Finally, when she knew she'd done all she could, she moved back from Drew. He carefully pulled his jacket back over her shoulders. Her breasts felt incredibly sensitive, almost burning, but there was no time to explore the implications of what this might mean.

"We are masked -- for now," she said on a ragged breath. "A small protection." She met his eyes. "Drive as fast as you dare to this Dell's Bridge." She swallowed. "I promise not to interfere in your driving of this vehicle."

Drew cleared his throat, moving on the seat uncomfortably, but remained silent as he turned his attention to driving and they moved quickly down the road.

"Can you go faster?" she fretted, staring straight ahead. "As soon as we arrive, you must leave. You might be able to avoid danger."

His large hands gripped the wheel. "I'm not leaving you out there in the road."

"There will be someone there," she said quietly. "However, if we don't get there before the elder the decision may be taken from us."

"I don't understand any of this, Pandimora. What just happened? It looked like electricity arcing around us." He gripped the wheel. "At least tell me what you expect to find out there."

"Faeries who can help."

"Faeries," he muttered.

"Yes, in a special healing sanctuary. In Aisywel, I witnessed an elder strike down another faerie. Unlike humans, faeries are immortal. However, in rare instances a faerie can be sent away as punishment. Being immortal, they would live out their days away from our faerie realms. It is a terrible thing and as far as I was aware, has only happened rarely in faerie history. When the elder discovered I'd been listening and saw everything, he tried to mind wash me so I would forget. But I remembered! I fled." A deep ache twisted inside. "I should have stayed and tried to alert the elder high council and also find my sister, but I ran away."

Surprisingly, he reached for her hand. Pandimora liked the feeling of his hand engulfing her own. "Does your sister know what's happened?" he asked.

"I don't know. I hope her ignorance will provide protection." With difficulty, she drew in a deep breath. Her chest hurt. "At Dell's Bridge there is a portal to a healing realm. I can get well and go back for my sister."

"There's a healing realm out there in the middle of nowhere?" His voice sounded skeptical. He didn't believe her. "Why out there?"

"The area has a unique geology of quartz and magnetic lodestone and in combination with the sulfur springs, it is a vortex of spiraling energies that exists through many dimensions. There are few places in any of the worlds that offer such a unique blend of energy."

"How will you be safe if the elder comes after you?"

"The healing realm is a dimension removed from Aisywel and therefore somewhat hidden. It is the only safe place. There is no other choice."

"How will you get into this place if the elder is waiting?"

She knew he was right. The elder could outpace her and always be one step ahead. How could she really hide?

As they moved through the night, Pandimora saw the reflection of her white face in the mirror. Guilt weighed on her. She had abandoned her sister and now Drew was in danger.

She pressed a hand to her head. Maybe none of this was happening as she'd thought. The pain in her head and shoulder made it hard to concentrate. Even though the wounds appeared to have healed on the outside, she could feel the tendrils of poison working inside.

She had to remain strong in her convictions, remember who she was ... remember what had happened.

She could still feel the intensity of the raw energy she and Drew had exchanged. His human scent felt stronger all around her in the vehicle, and it was on her skin also. She had to force herself not to lean heavily into him again. In these modern times such an energy exchange with a human was forbidden because as time went on their worlds grew further apart. She had known Drew a long time, but sadly it was not unusual for humans to forget the faeries they used to know as children. Human memory at times had its own cloaking device, shielding humans from memories that might prove overwhelming or too fantastic for them to believe. She had known Drew and his brother since they were young boys. She and her sister had played with them all one summer.

She hugged her arms around herself. The more time he spent with her, the more she endangered him.

Pandimora bit her lips on a groan as needles of pain sliced her. Pain was foreign to faeries, but she had observed enough humans in pain to know it for what it was. It wound around each cell, infiltrating her entire body.

Drew threw her a glance. "We're almost there."

Her vision seemed to be failing and she feared her body was shutting down.

And what if these were her last moments? It was possible she could die from the evil poisoning her body and not even the healing sanctuary could make her well. Lukais's magic could prove stronger than her immortality.

She would never see Drew again. Her breath caught in sadness. Knowing this would be her last contact with him, Pandimora reached up and gently touched the back of her hand to his hard jaw with its soft growth of stubble. He was a human, but she was fond of him as she thought of the memories of their summer together.

"I'm sorry you've become involved in this," she said softly.

Drew looked at her, his handsome face expressing concern. "We're here," he said gruffly, and stopped the vehicle in the middle of the road. The wind seemed to pick up in ferocity as it rocked the large vehicle."There's nothing here," he said flatly, looking out the window.

Pandimora opened the truck door.

"Wait!" he said. "You have bare feet --"

She evaded his hand and quickly slid off the seat to the snowy road. "The portal." A gentle blue and gold glow hung suspended in the air. The activated portal. Drew hurried to her side, putting an arm around her waist as she swayed.

"No one's here," he said louder as the wind whipped them.

She pointed to the faint glow, not sure if he could see it in the swirling snow. The wind stilled for a moment and the arm around her tensed.

"Geez," he muttered. "Geez." Disbelief on his face.

"There's a dark cloud or something coming," he said grimly, staring over his shoulder into the darkness.

"Your realm is dense and that has worked to our advantage. Drew, there is no way to show my deep thanks, but you must go!"

The portal flickered and snapped as if the energy flow had been interrupted. As she stepped toward it a little man suddenly leapt from the portal and rolled onto the snowy ground beside them. He jumped to his feet.

"Finally!" he yelled, grabbing her arm. "Hurry! I can't hold the energy much longer."

Pandimora recognized his light energy as belonging to her world.

"You're the guy in the road!" Drew exclaimed. "Let go of her." He held her back.

"It's okay," Pandimora said, trying to step away from him.

The faerie tugged her forward, his energy all encompassing and no match for a human's. Pandimora entered the portal with Drew still holding on to her.

"No!" shouted the other man, but it was too late.

All three of them were sucked into the portal.

∞ Chapter Three ∞

Pandimora lay curled on the ground, brilliant green ferns cushioning her body. A heavy mist hung all around her, the air lit by brilliant fireflies. Not the scarlet and gold fireflies she knew from home but equally beautiful blue and green fireflies.

"Pandimora." The little man's voice came to her, although she could not see him. "Go to the healing springs to be cleansed of the black poison. Go now." She felt his concern in the air around her.

She felt a nudge against her arm, then against her leg. The heavy mist clung to her, warming her where she lay, but her mind felt sluggish and she didn't move.

"Get up, get up," female voices said behind her. Small winged creatures floated in and out of her line of vision.

"Who are you?" Pandimora clenched her jaw, digging her fingers into the soft ground as she struggled upright.

The creatures flew around her head and then in front of her face. The smaller of the creatures came very close. She had yellow hair and frowned fiercely, her purple gossamer wings beating the air with a slight hum. "We are trying to help you."

"Immerse yourself in the water." The second faerie flew down near her legs and pinched her skin when Pandimora did not move.

"Ouch."

"Hurry. Into the healing springs. Your body is dying from the inside."

Pandimora managed to get to her knees, and then slowly to her feet, frightened by the weak tremble of her legs. Every part of her body ached with terrible pain. Her thoughts were also jumbled inside her head. She could catch a thought now and then, but each time it quickly flitted away.

The two creatures gently urged her across soft moss, the woods semi-dark and yet welcoming. The trees held shadowy arms out to her and seemed to sigh as she passed, but she felt their sadness also. The area ahead began to glow with vibrant, bubbling light. When she thought she could walk no more, they entered a small clearing.

The charged, sparkling air looked very much like Aisywel. She reached out to touch a faerie light, but it flitted away from her and into the arms of the sheltering trees. "Am I home, then?" she asked in wonder.

"This is an Aisywel simulation. You can never go home," the first creature said sadly.

A small pool of water lay before her, emerald

green with tiny curls of silver sparkles drifting from the water's surface.

She turned. "Why can't I go home?"

The second creature hovered in front of her. "You are banished," she said, pointing to the many-pointed star on Pandimora's arm. "You were marked for protection, but now the star has been altered," the little creature added in a hushed whisper. She held out her tiny hand, and Pandimora saw a similar many-pointed star on her palm. "As we bear the mark of banishment we also are banned from Aisywel."

"Why are you banished?" she asked.

Impatiently, the yellow haired faerie nudged her forward. "This healing realm is your only opportunity to relieve your body of the killing poison. Utilize this spring to get well. We will hope it is not too late."

Pandimora looked around, catching a thought and holding onto it. "Where is Drew? He came with me."

"The human is under observation. Is he yours?" asked the yellow haired faerie with a slight giggle.

Pandimora looked at her, trying to focus. "Mine? No, of course not." No, she would in time find a faerie mate, not a human. She frowned, unsuccessfully trying to shake her foggy confusion. "I need to hide."

"You are safe here," said the yellow-haired creature, her voice now soothing and warm. "Remain in these magical springs until the wounds no longer fester and burn. There now, go gently."

Pandimora tried to shake off her blouse, difficult

due to the ache in her arms, but the winged creatures pulled the blouse easily over her head and let it drop to the mossy ground, then pushed the silky pants down her legs. She stepped into the spring, which was hot on her naked flesh, but not unpleasantly so. Letting her eyes drift closed, she ducked down until the water covered her to her chin. As the water soaked into her skin, it began to sting, invading every pore as its healing properties scrubbed her, relentless in its pursuit of the poison.

The water around her gradually grew murky and cool. As she began to shiver, the two faeries urged her from the water. Looking down at her body she was horrified to see black liquid seeping like blood from the pores of her skin. She twisted to look back at the pool and saw that it, too, was now black.

They brought her to a second pool, this one glistening blue like the tropical waters of Aisywel. Her breath caught as she entered the water, sadness heavy upon her that she would never return to her birthplace. She looked at the mark on her arm. Her mother Clare had marked her for protection, but after her encounter with Lukais, the star had changed. The thought that she couldn't return home was a fresh misery heaped upon her physical pain.

The water stung once again, until it felt as if her blood boiled and sharp talons ripped at her insides. She tried to remain still, but the pain caused tears to flow from her eyes as she writhed in agony.

"I never cry," she said, pushing away the wetness on her cheeks.

"There was a time you cried," said the yellow-haired creature, her voice hushed.

"No. I don't remember."

"It was a long time ago, when your mother left."

The tears continued to stream down her cheeks, coloring the water around her.

Pandimora went still. "Did you know my mother Clare?"

"All knowledge in the faerie worlds is shared, even though much time has passed. You will find your own memories in time." Pandimora put her hand up to wipe her eyes, and her fingers came away black. She looked up at the hovering yellow-haired faerie.

"Do not be afraid, it is the poison being purged from your body," the faerie assured her.

Gradually the tears ceased, but the pain continued, and she must have passed out briefly because she came to with a start, her arms flailing, splashing the water as the faeries held her head above water. Immediately she went still and thanked them humbly.

Gradually the deep soreness inside began to be soothed away. The water around her cleared, no longer colored by the black tears but once more a deep, healing blue. Pandimora felt the water's energy as it embraced and cushioned her with great care. The pool began to bubble and sparkle brightly. Looking all around, Pandimora wished she could take joy in the absolute splendor of her surroundings, but a curious numbness hung on her. She couldn't even appreciate the silvery leaves which glittered upon nearby trees or the purple stemmed mushrooms growing along the water's edge, which she loved to eat.

The winged creatures left her, riding a wave of light as great blue and white plumes of faerie dust swirled in the air. As the miracle of the mineral waters began to fully revive her, Pandimora's thoughts reorganized and gained clarity. But where was Drew?

He had come through the portal with her, but beyond that she did not remember anything. Pandimora shook her hair back as it fell into her eyes. Gingerly, she touched her temple then moved her fingers carefully over the diminished soreness on the right side of her head, rubbing gently, trying to ease a slight ache behind her right eye. As reluctant as she was to delve into the fear which still swirled within, she knew she must uncover the memory of what had occurred when she fled Aisywel. It was crucial to her survival that she remember everything.

Taking a deep breath, she closed her eyes and beckoned to the memories. They came dancing like the shadows of a dream.

She'd overheard the elder Lukais arguing with another faerie and in the end the other faerie had been struck down and then engulfed by a green mist until he disappeared. Pandimora hadn't believed her eyes. Lukais had always been a mentor to her and her sister while growing up. She'd tried to run away, but Lukais had seen her. He'd tried to make her forget but she'd remembered.

Pandimora materialized a portal and fled through it, transporting to the small cottage where she and Lilja lived. Her breath came fast, heart beating in panic. She had to find her sister so they could flee.

Lukais as an elder was well versed in all the magic Aisywel held. But, although she knew herself to be no match for his dexterity, she had to try to evade him.

Her mind raced. She would never see another sunrise on Aisywel, the realm of her birth. Why must she continually question what other faeries accepted? Other faeries never asserted independent ways or defied the elders by sneaking into the earth dimension. If she had not eavesdropped none of this would have happened. How could she fix this so it would all go away?

Her bright red hair flew into her eyes and she pushed it back, jumping into one last portal and running toward the turquoise lake with its silver edging. Legs shaking, her chest heaved as her momentum took her to the edge of the lake. Why couldn't she find her sister? Where could they go that he could not follow? Aisywel had always been her life, and now it no longer felt safe.

She braced her feet near the lake's edge, fear holding her rigid. The elder now stood behind her. Lukais put up a calming hand. "Pandimora, how dramatically you are reacting to what you mistakenly think you saw."

"A faerie lay on the ground. I saw the mist take him." Never had she so blatantly defied an elder. "I heard what you planned, how you wish to control all the universe's resources for your own use. How can that not be evil?"

He stepped closer and she retreated, the lake water warm around her bare ankles. In this beautiful paradise, she felt cornered.

"Come away, there is no need for alarm. You have misunderstood."

"You are lying."

"Lying is a grave charge to level at an elder," he mused.

"Striking a faerie is a terrible thing." She retreated another step into the water, pressing a hand to her stomach.

"There is harm in your false accusation, Pandimora. It saddens me that I will, of course, have to report this to the high elder council."

Pandimora shivered. She could be punished ... exiled from her beloved Aisywel.

"There is no evidence of wrong doing on my part," Lukais continued, watching her with sadness. He held out his slim hand. "Come. I will speak to the council on your behalf."

Her life was ruined, out of perfect balance. All she thought she knew about Aisywel was tainted.

"You are acting like an earth being, all due to a misunderstanding." He waved his stick. "Look around. All is still splendid, despite the aberration of your mind and thoughts."

The question gave her pause and she felt a hint of uncertainty. "I know what I saw." She crossed her arms but seeds of doubt had crept in.

"What you think you saw," he corrected her gently. "Pandimora, I have always cared about you and your sister. You must trust me now."

She had an almost irresistible urge to close her eyes in acquiescence, but struggled to remain alert. "I - I'm confused."

"We have nurtured you here in Aisywel. I thought perhaps with time you would outgrow the need to hide and listen to private conversations."

She watched him warily.

"You never outgrew that human habit." His mouth grew tight and she watched his fingers grip the wooden staff. "You are very like your mother," he added.

"What do you know of my mother?" She felt the hopeful, trembling note in her own voice. She knew little of her parents. A secret wish, long buried, surfaced. She had longed to have parents as the humans did. She had never told anyone, not even her sister.

Now he looked thoughtful, a slight regret on his face. "Clare came to Aisywel long ago at my invitation. I had hoped our world would have a calming effect on her." He stared up at the perfect blue sky. "She suffered episodes due to a mental disorder that jumbled her thoughts. She ran away one night, abandoning her children and her husband, my dear friend Declan."

Pandimora caught her breath, deep pain lancing her.

"You were very young." He looked down at her from his greater height. "Giving birth to your sister must have snapped Clare's mind. She ran off shortly thereafter."

Her chin trembled but she clenched her teeth so she didn't cry.

"We thought it best to shield you from this tragedy. Both your parents disappeared that night." He turned so she could no longer see his face but his words pierced her heart, opening a desire long hidden. Humans had family units, something that had drawn her to them. She'd had a family and never known! An ache twisted inside, a feeling of being abandoned.

"I searched a long time, but my dear friend Declan was gone."

The heaviness in her chest intensified. She bit her lip, worrying it between her teeth until she tasted the saltiness of blood. Faeries almost never bled. She touched a finger to her lip, stared at it.

"The high council placed you and your sister in the faerie nursery and erased from your experience the loss of your parents."

Panic twisted through Pandimora, making it difficult to focus. "If my mother came to Aisywel at your invitation, from which faerie realm did she come?"

"Not faerie," he said, giving her a piercing stare. "Clare was human."

Human! She shook her head no.

Pandimora put her arms around her stomach, feeling betrayed.

"Come, I will show you," he said solemnly.

Lukais withdrew a vibrant green crystal from deep within a robe pocket. She had heard of the beauty of the Aisywel crystals, but she'd never actually seen one. It was magnificent, a rod about the length of his palm and it shot sparks and iridescent light all around them, drawing upon the color of the sky and the glittering quartz stones along the water's edge. Lukais used the crystal to draw circles before him in the air. The precious jewel created thin trails of pure gold light and a holographic scene began to form between them.

"You know about the life force of the crystals," he said. "Did you also know the crystals cannot lie?"

Pandimora watched intently as a young woman appeared in the holographic scene. She looked about her own age and had long, curling red hair. But the woman also had a wildness in her blue eyes that was painful to see. Pandimora swallowed as the woman turned her head from side to side, as if looking for someone. She couldn't take her eyes from the hologram as she drank in every detail.

"Declan!" Pandimora stepped back when the woman screamed the name. Again, she screamed out, "Declan!"

Pandimora saw herself, a young child and her sister, an infant swaddled in a shimmering blue cloth. The woman cried uncontrollably as she opened an intricately carved wooden cabinet, urged Pandimora inside and then placed her sister in her young arms. The woman mouthed strange, fevered words and pressed her fingers upon Pandimora's arm. When she drew back, Pandimora saw the elven star on her skin.

Her mother exposed her sister's tiny shoulder, tears streaming down her face as she again mouthed fevered words. A triskele with its three interlocked spirals appeared on her sister's shoulder. Just as she closed the cabinet door on them, Pandimora saw a dark-haired young man appear behind the woman. The image dissolved.

"Wait!" Pandimora yearned to know more.

"Your mother was disturbed," Lukais said. "She

hid you and fled. We did not know your whereabouts for several days as she put both you and Lilja into a deep sleep. When you awoke we felt it best to erase your memories."

"Why are you telling me this now?" She bit the inside of her cheek, her world turned upside down. Her parents had abandoned them? A terrible emptiness pervaded her soul.

"It was time for you to understand that only in Aisywel can you be understood."

Pandimora wanted to see her mother again, but right now she was hardly able to take in what she had seen. She focused on the one thing she knew was real. "What happened to the faerie in the garden?" She couldn't stop her body from shaking.

"You had an hallucination just as your mother used to suffer. I had hoped you would not inherit her madness."

Fear twisted a knot in her stomach."I am not my mother," she managed, ashamed there was no real challenge in her voice.

"Humans carry anomalies from one generation to the next. Did you ever wonder why you are different from other faeries? Always seeking answers to questions others never ask? Never content with what Aisywel offers. Always fascinated by the earth realm."

A deep buzzing began in her ears, its force making her sway on her feet.

"Pandimora, be calm," he said. "Do not do this to yourself." His voice was above her.

Her breath came faster and her heart worked in her chest. "I'm not doing anything," she said.

"You're projecting your energy toward me and I have no choice but to block it. It is the gravest offense to try to manipulate an elder with the force of your life energy."

Blue light snapped between them and she cried out as molten heat scorched her right temple, then moved over her shoulder and burned its way down her arm. Her sacred elven star became a burning welt. All these years she had never known why only she and her sister had these marks. Now she knew her mother had marked them, but why?

"Make it stop."

Lukais stepped back. "I am sorry it has to be like this, but I must protect Aisywel."

Pandimora stumbled into the lake. For the first time in her life she knew weakness in her limbs. Her skin burned; the pain was debilitating.

"Stop," he said aloud. "You are harming yourself."

She choked as water flowed into her mouth. She had but an instant's reprieve before the razor-sharp light struck her shoulder again.

Was she creating this terrible pain that now ripped through her body?

She flailed her arms, turned and swam down into the lake, afraid she might drown. The pain in her scalp burned like fire, as if her head were engulfed in flames. Frantically, her thoughts turned to Lilja. Was her sister afflicted with the same illness?

With her lungs bursting she kept diving down. Black wisps of smoke followed her, twisting around her. On the lake bottom she saw a blue portal. Black wispy fingers of smoke gripped the tender flesh of her feet like steel claws, then bound her ankles, circling around and encasing her legs and knees, reaching up to her shoulders. This couldn't be her doing! Why would she harm herself?

She touched the portal. The black tendrils tugged at her, pointed barbs digging into her flesh. As the poison seeped in from the barbs, her brain began to fog over, the pain in her head so intense, she could barely think. In a last attempt to save herself, she desperately clutched the edges of the portal, wriggling her legs so that her pants were ripped away, and then her blouse tore from her shoulders.

She put all her energy into pulling herself through the portal, pushed her shoulders through and her head was out on the other side where she pulled in deep gulps of cold air. She dug her elbows into the edges of the portal as the black mass tried to pull her back.

She kicked her bound legs, using the force of the water to propel herself through the portal, landing on cold, snowy ground.

The pain in her head exploded and she screamed.

***

Pandimora jerked her head back, opening her eyes when the memory finished playing. But was it the true memory of what had occurred or had the part of her that could harbor human illness created its own story as Lukais had suggested?

Panic wound through her. Lukais had allowed the crystal to show her the family she had forgotten. Had she been thrust from Aisywel to protect the realm or had she really seen something he wanted to remain hidden?

Pandimora left the healing spring, warm air circulating around her as she stepped carefully upon the springy moss underfoot. She lifted her arms and clothing materialized upon her body. She drew in several deep breaths, thankful to be vibrantly whole again. The pain was gone and her skin glowed with health once more. Her mind and body continued the healing as she slowly began to feel back to her normal self.

Knowing what she must do, Pandimora materialized a portal, light blue in this healing sanctuary with silver and white edges. She looked deep into the portal, seeing her home Aisywel just on the other side. All she had to do was step inside, but she lingered a moment, for once in her life afraid as she stared into the world that had birthed and nurtured her all her many years. Happy years, yes, but many times a sense of being different had been a part of her. All this time she'd thought her parents gone from their lives due to natural causes. But now, it appeared something terrible may have happened.

She needed to get her sister to safety. She stepped through the portal and into Aisywel, but her feet met only air and she immediately began to fall into a vast nothingness.

Pandimora screamed, managed to grasp the portal edges. Breathing hard, she looked down at the emptiness below. With immense effort, using her hands and then her elbows for support, she pulled herself back up into the portal and lay across the threshold, feeling a stiff breeze pulsing from below, pulling at her feet and legs. It swirled all around her, as if trying to suck her down into the emptiness.

She pulled herself back into the sanctuary and the portal dissolved on its own. She lay with her cheek against the moss, fighting back the tears. It was true, then. For her, there was no Aisywel. It did not exist for a faerie exiled. She was truly lost to her own kind.

∞ Chapter Four ∞

Drew struggled but was unable to move. Standing in the same spot where he'd entered this place with Pandimora and the little man, his feet felt like they were stuck to the ground. "Hey!" he called, looking up. "Is anybody there?"

Drew was still disbelieving of his surroundings. Wherever he was, everything looked so perfect as to be unreal. The trees in front of him had no dead limbs or off color leaves and the actual color of the bark and leaves was unreal, almost a barrage to his brain since everything was bright and vibrant with life. The moss beneath him was green and springy. Flowers grew along the clearing where he stood in a multitude of colors, some of which he wasn't sure he could even name. He supposed if this was a faerie dimension, he couldn't have dreamed it any better. The air felt a perfect temperature, much more comfortable than the snow and the swiftly dropping temperature where he'd last been. Pandimora had claimed it was a healing sanctuary. Was he really in another dimension, or was it merely an area that had been carefully staged?

A shiver raced up Drew's neck as he heard a distant scream. Was that Pandimora? He struggled to no avail.

He felt something hard at his back and turned his head to see a large tree. Then a chain appeared across his chest. Cursing, he immediately pushed and tugged at the heavy chain as it tightened.

"It will do no good," said a male voice. Drew looked to see the little man who'd pulled Pandimora into the portal. The same one who had stood in the road. About four and a half feet tall, he wore a long sleeved green shirt and black pants with a green vertical stripe down the sides. On his feet he wore black sneakers.

"You almost made me go into a ditch with your stunt in the road," Drew said. "What the heck was that about?"

"I needed you to stop and turn around."

"We could have crashed."

"You didn't. You shouldn't have taken her away."

"How was I to know that? She was in a blinding snowstorm with no protection. Where am I?"

"The healing dimension."

Drew sighed. "Listen, let me go. This isn't necessary." He tugged at the chain.

"We were never introduced," said the man. He bowed in an almost courtly manner. "I'm Irfin."

Drew stopped struggling, staring at the man. "Drew Maddox."

"I know who you are." Irfin looked off into the trees where the light continually changed, varying between dawn and dusk and then an inky twilight. Drew had seen it when he first arrived and just figured someone had a dimmer switch.

"Why this elaborate setup?" Drew asked. "It's a little over the top."

"Do you think so?" The man Irfin smiled. "Thank you."

"It wasn't necessarily a compliment. Did you hear that scream? Is Pandimora all right?" Drew asked.

The man stood tensely for several moments, and then he seemed to relax. His mid-length brown hair stuck out from his head as if he'd pulled it with his fingers.

When Drew had seen him trying to pull Pandimora through some type of lit doorway, he'd reacted instinctively. Little had he known he'd end up a captive in a strange place where nothing matched the world as he knew it. Was he really in a fantasy faerie world? With all the strange things that had been happening, he had a hard time figuring out any of this.

"Don't worry yourself," said Irfin. "All is well. Sometimes it's difficult for humans to believe such a place, or faeries, exist."

Drew stared at Irfin as he sat down, a short stump appearing behind him.

Drew frowned. "How can all be well?" he asked. "Everything here is too perfect, too staged, as if we're in a play and everything is in place."

"On the contrary, this is the real world. Your

earth dimension is the stage."

"I suppose next you'll say we're all puppets?"

"I would never say that."

"Release me so I can go find her," Drew said, staring at Irfin as he pulled a tied piece of red string from his pocket. Drew remembered as a kid playing cat's cradle string games, but he'd always played with a second person, usually his sister Pam. Now, Irfin was playing string games all by himself, the colored string suspended in mid-air before him.

"How can you do cat's cradle with one person?" Drew asked, irritated the man ignored his requests to be released.

Irfin looked up at him and grinned. "There is more here than meets the eye."

Drew watched as invisible fingers appeared to work the strings opposite him, ending up with the string in intricate diamond shapes. "Ask Pandimora," he said. "She'll confirm I've been helping her."

"I don't know the circumstances of that, seeing as how you jumped the portal without permission," Irfin said in his lilting voice. "You will have to be patient." The man discarded the string. "If Pandimora corroborates your story, you will be released and sent back."

"She looked in a bad way. I'd rather go to her and see if she needs my help."

Irfin smirked. "I don't think you'll be able to help her as much as the magic of the fae."

"What harm can I do if you release me? It's not like I'm familiar with this place. I don't even know how to get out of here."

Irfin raised a brow and he chuckled, his small

beard wobbling. "What harm, he says. What harm. A human could wreak terrible havoc in such a magical place."

"At least I'm trying to help. By the look of it, no one else has been helping Pandimora."

Irfin narrowed his eyes. "What are you saying?"

"She was attacked and no one did a thing to help her."

"It may appear that way, but you, being a human, don't understand the logistics of a magical faerie world."

"Why don't you explain the logistics? It seems I have time on my hands." He needed as much information as possible.

"Well, now, when a human enters the healing sanctuary, they have access to the same knowledge as any other faerie while here. You no doubt saw the attack on Pandimora as she relived it?"

"I saw the attack on her, it was like a -- a movie screen in front of me." He was still a bit shaken over what he'd seen, the old guy throwing what looked like bolts of electric at her as she tried to get away. It made him even more determined to find her. In fact, to Drew, the entire movie experience had seemed like science fiction, but it had also seemed all too real. "Tell me about the elder who attacked her. The one who's still after her."

"That must be sorted out," Irfin said stiffly. "A high elder is over a thousand years old. You don't just accuse him of treachery. There must be a hearing, the facts submitted."

"Meanwhile, I'm assuming he would cover his tracks and clean up his mess."

Irfin's eyes flashed with annoyance. "An elder is not like your politicians. He is an esteemed individual with special powers granted him by the crystals he safe-keeps."

"What are the crystals?"

"The powerful eyes of nature. They keep all worlds operating properly. Physically, they generally measure no longer than a man's palm, but they have an intuitive knowledge about all worlds. They were forged in ancient times from the fires deep beneath the earth's core." Drew heard a sense of pride in Irfin's voice.

"And one person controls these powerful crystals? I have to wonder at giving one person so much power. I presume he comes and goes as he pleases. Perhaps everyone in your world can be kept in ignorance if he decides to shield his less than desirable activities --"

Irfin put up a hand and cut him off. "There are other factors involved. It has not been determined if the high elder did indeed act maliciously or in self-defense. Until we know everything, there will be no judgments made."

"You're supposedly helping Pandimora get well, and yet you're defending this guy -- this Lukais --"

"Ack!" With alarm tightening his face, Irfin threw up a hand. "It is disrespectful for a human to speak an elder's name."

"Okay, this elder then, who may or may not have taken the life of another faerie. Pandimora saw something, then the elder comes after her."

"According to Pandimora's account."

Drew narrowed his eyes. "Don't you believe her?

Can these videos or whatever it was be edited?"

"You are not in a movie theater! And it is not up to me to believe her." But Irfin avoided looking at him.

"Then who is in charge in this place?"

Impatiently, Irfin stood, hands on hips. "There is no one in charge. This sanctuary is a collective effort of many energies."

"I saw what those pictures, like a movie playing in the air. I saw what Pandimora experienced as, apparently, so did you. How can you doubt she's innocent?"

"You were not there," Irfin said, "so you are not one to judge."

"Do you think she fabricated it? This is all too crazy."

"Hmph -- you've known Pandimora how long?"

"It doesn't matter. I'm a trained cop and now a private investigator with ten years collective experience. You get to know people in that line of work." But even he was feeling skeptical about this entire set up since he'd found her in the road.

Irfin sighed. "Be assured Pandimora will be protected until all the facts are known."

"That sounds wishy-washy to me," Drew said harshly.

"Perhaps. But as you implied reality can be distorted or changed. And the fact is Pandimora is different from most faeries."

Drew arched a brow. Anything about Pandimora intrigued him. He focused back on the task, his investigative instincts kicking in.

"Her heritage is unique," Irfin continued. "She

has great curiosity about your race and explores your world as she pleases, much to the displeasure of the elders. She also eavesdrops on conversations. That is how she overheard this exchange between the faerie and the elder."

Drew shrugged. "Seems to me pretty harmless, living as you choose to live, following your interests. It only becomes dangerous when a society bans independence and free thinkers. Who is going to protect her from the elder?"

Irfin looked at him in surprise. "She has not asked for protection. She intends to find the truth of what happened to her family."

Alarm snaked through Drew. "Is she going back to this Aisywel?"

"If Pandimora wishes you to know, she will tell you."

Drew pushed against the chain impatiently.

Irfin watched, rubbing his chin thoughtfully. "Patience," he said. He stood and sauntered back and forth across the mossy ground as if he had all the time in the world. In his hand appeared a bright orange yo-yo. He unreeled it then pulled it back up toward him. "It's highly unusual for a human to penetrate our sanctuary without an invitation," he said, walking the yo-yo on the ground.

Irfin expertly swung the yo-yo in an arc, performing tricks as it sailed over his head and rolled down his arm, then he quickly caught it on the string and bounced it back and forth between his hands. Swinging it out in front of him, Irfin brought it back under his leg and then over his head.

Drew put his head back against the tree and

gently hit his head against the bark a few times. Nope, he wasn't dreaming, he was really here, watching a so-called faerie perform intricate yo-yo tricks. Could this all be true?

As the light faded a little, fireflies began to appear. One flew around his head, then back and forth and paused in front of him, similar to the way a hummingbird would hover in the air.

Drew stared into a pair of eyes that looked vaguely human. "Geez!" It was swiftly gone.

Irfin looked at him, one brow cocked.

"I thought it was a bug," he muttered. "I'm glad I didn't swat it as it flew by my face. I could have killed it."

Irfin laughed, his puckish face and wide mouth making him look like a storybook elf. "You would have received an unpleasant jolt of electricity if you'd tried," he said, then cocked his head, listening.

"Is Pandimora coming?" He wished he knew if she was okay. When they'd entered this place things had gone fuzzy, but he wasn't exactly sure for how long. When he'd come to, she was gone.

"What did he do to her, exactly?"

"Black tendrils of poison must be purged from her system."

Drew felt an escalation of alarm. "And you still think this guy might be innocent? And what about the black strips of material that had been bound around her legs? How can you defend someone who would do that to a woman?" He studied the other man but could see no reaction. "And now I'm in this secret world -- a world within worlds," he muttered. "From what I've seen of you faeries, you could just as easily use mind control instead something as old fashioned as a chain."

Irfin lifted his head and threw back his shoulders. "I will forgive your faux pas this time, but I will tell you only once. I am of the fae, but I am not faerie."

"Okay," Drew said, confused.

"I claim leprechaun as my birthright and I will abide no snide remarks about leprechauns and their pots of gold. I am from a long line of sorcerers."

"A sorcerer?" Drew sighed. "I really am not up on my leprechaun or faerie history. I didn't realize a leprechaun could also be a sorcerer."

"From ancient times there were many clans with pure and distinct family lines. However, the last three centuries the lines have intermingled and blurred. I claim birthright to the first true line of leprechauns."

Drew cocked a brow. "And you also have some kind of power to keep me immobilized?"

"It is an ancient power wielded around humans when the necessity arises."

"So with your powers there's really no need for you to be worried about me damaging anything in this place. Release me," Drew said again.

Irfin shook his head. "Ach, no. We will wait for Pandimora to return." And Irfin sat down once more, staring with narrowed eyes at Drew as he stuffed the bright yo-yo back in his pocket. When he pulled his hand out of the pocket, it was clenched around something else.

Drew crossed his arms over his chest. Irfin opened his fist and dropped several colored, multi-pointed jacks on the stone at his feet.

"Don't you get bored playing games and being stuck on prisoner duty?" he asked as the other man bounced a small red ball and swiped a hand through the jacks to pick them up, then caught the rubber ball again. Irfin tried again but, unable to pick up even one of the multi-pointed jacks, he began to look frustrated.

Irfin gave him his attention, one brow raised. "Who says I'm here all day? And why would I be bored?" he added, surprised. "Boredom comes with idle hands. Mine, as well you see, are never idle. And do not think of yourself as a prisoner." He smiled with great charm. "Think of yourself as a guest in our world." He lifted a brow. "Why were you driving out in this fairly desolate area so late at night?"

"I'm a private investigator. I drive all over on cases." Drew didn't intend to tell him he had been on his way to meet with his client Mrs. Palmer. Instead, he remarked, "Where I come from we don't chain our guests to a tree."

"Hmm." Irfin looked thoughtful as he bounced the ball again and managed to grab one jack. "You've never handcuffed a man to a fence, or chased another man through the woods and tackled him around the legs? And what about throwing sand in some hapless fellow's face? I suppose you've never done any of those things, now have you?"

A twitching began between his shoulders. How did Irfin know any of that? "That was all in the line of duty, protecting myself or innocent bystanders before anyone could get hurt. Those men weren't my guests; they had hurt innocent people."

"Ach, so you say."

"Yeah, and I'm sure you also know the circumstances surrounding those events," Drew said dismissively. He had to wonder though how Irfin knew any of that. It had all occurred during his time as a cop. "So what do you do when you're not playing games or spying into human's lives?" he asked.

"I live my life, just as you do."

Drew remained still. "Down here in this place?" Wherever this place was. As far as he knew he could be in some type of underground bunker.

Irfin suddenly dropped the ball and the jacks. "Ach, I give up." He stood and walked away. Drew read the frustration in the stiff set of Irfin's shoulders. Apparently, frustration was similar in his world or theirs.

Drew called after him. "Release me and I'll show you how to win."

Irfin spun on his heel and gave him an assessing glance. "Mmm. That's a tempting offer," he said, rubbing his hand over his short beard. "Very tempting, but probably just a bluff. It's really not about winning, it's about playing."

"I know how to play," Drew said.

Irfin lifted a brow. "Really? Humans are preoccupied with work and have lost much of the ability to play."

"I've played with my niece. We call it jacks."

"A child's past time," said Irfin, nodding. "When I was a child, we called it knucklebones." He sighed, staring off into the forest around them, a somewhat pensive air about him. "Innocent times long past. So much has changed between then and now." He threw Drew a look from under bushy brows. "Long ago, humans would never have been allowed to linger here. We would have scuttled you back to your own realm with nary a hair out of place. You would have woken in the morning and thought it all a dream."

"And why is now different?" Drew asked, curious.

He jerked his chin toward the forest. "Because of Pandimora. There's a cord of attachment between you."

"What does that mean?" Drew asked, an image of a silver cord connecting them through time and space popping into his head. He shook that notion aside. When had he gotten fanciful, for heaven's sake?

"You should use your imagination," Irfin said dryly. "When faerie or human meet someone and there's an attraction, a cord of attachment forms between those individuals. It is not something that can be lightly dismissed, not until the attraction has been played out -- or death occurs. But similar to your human life, even after death a silken strand remains with you."

Suddenly looking very somber, Irfin walked away, under the undulating arch of light brown tree limbs and through a low hanging mist. A narrow golden beam lit his path as a multitude of quickly moving fireflies swarmed the ground ahead of him.

Drew went back over all Irfin had said and wondered was it simply as he said, a healing sanctuary, or was there more to it?

He began to work at the chain again, sliding it sideways little by little. He hoped to find a lock that he could pick or a weakness in the chain. Intent, he kept turning the chain, and blew a breath upwards as sweat ran down, tickling his nose. After some time, however, he finally came to the realization the chain had no beginning or end. It was a continuous link.

"Drew!"

He looked up in relief to hear Pandimora's voice. She approached, clothed in an ivory short sleeved top and matching pants that reached her calves. Her bright blue eyes were clear and free of pain and confusion. Her deep red hair was on top of her head, glistening with tiny drops of moisture. Her feet were bare, her skin had an intriguing blush of color, as if touched by the sun.

He was immediately reminded of when he'd held her earlier, the strange sense of magic she'd exuded. He felt again the incredible sensation of her skin against his and remembered the weird blue light that had woven around them. He'd felt like a teenage boy again as he'd held her close, clearly able to hear her steady heart beat. Everything about her looked alive, fresh. Exotic.

Uncomfortably, he reminded himself he was a thirty-year old adult not an impressionable kid. "You look as if you feel better," he said, forgetting about the chain for a moment.

She nodded. "I am lucky to be revived." She stood so close to him that he caught the unmistakable scent of fresh baked cookies. He was losing it for sure.

"The faerie creatures told me you were under observation," she said with surprise. "I did not know you would be restrained, Drew. I am sorry." She touched his shoulder with her hand.

"Yeah, Irfin's been observing me getting frustrated. Can you free me from this chain?" he asked. "I'm hoping you've got a key."

"Drew, you can free yourself," she said. He stared into her deep blue eyes, a slight dimple peaking in her left cheek. Despite her obvious distress at the chain, he now saw an entirely different woman who sparkled with radiance and health.

She clucked her tongue and pressed his shoulder. "Come, move forward to free yourself."

Drew looked down at the steel chain heavy against his chest.

"Look at the chain closely," she said patiently.

"I am. It's about three inches from my face."

"It's a chain of daisies," she said.

He scowled. "Pandimora, this is no time for jokes, really."

"Study it carefully."

He'd rather have looked at her, but he looked down at the chain as she had instructed. It was no longer made of heavy steel links but rather an interlocking chain of flowers, delicate flowers resembling daisies, except they were blue with red centers.

"What!" He moved forward and the flowers fell to his feet then dried up and melted into the ground.

She bent down toward the flowers. "Thank you, dear flowers, for your service," she said. "Now you may return to your duties in the forest."

Drew lifted a brow, hardly able to believe it all. "They held me captive."

She nodded seriously. "Yes, they have performed a task and it is necessary to thank them and show my appreciation, no matter the service provided."

"You're thanking them for pretending to be heavy steel chain," he muttered. "I am losing my mind."

"Drew, something you should never forget: what you expect to see in any faerie realm is what you will see. You felt yourself bound by something strong and of course you would not look at a daisy and see yourself held in place by daisies. It had to be something that you could not break, like a chain or a heavy rope. That is what you expected to see and that is what you saw."

"I will never live this down. Held captive by a chain of daisies. Did Irfin know?" At her shrug, he grunted. "Of course he did. No doubt he found it particularly amusing to see me struggling against a chain of daisies. He's a sorcerer playing psychological games. Either that or I'm losing my mind."

"You are not losing your mind. Leprechauns can sometimes be a mischievous lot," she conceded. "But he meant no real harm. He was helping to protect this sacred place."

Pandimora leaned in close, her fiery hair brushing his chin, then she tilted her chin back. Her nostrils flared, as if she were inhaling his scent. Drew held perfectly still, mesmerized. Irrationally, he thought he wouldn't mind if she took a bite out of him. Something intriguing about her wound all around him and he in turn leaned closer to her.

She touched his neck with cool fingers and the slight contact left him burning for more. Surprising him, she pressed her full red lips to his. Drew barely had a moment to savor the sensation before she pulled back.

She shrugged. "At times, my curiosity gets the best of me," she said.

He lifted a brow, wondering if she was up to something, but her face looked placid, innocent of guile. Or so it appeared.

"The bottom has truly fallen out of my entire world," she said. "Everything I know has been snatched away."

"You do seem to be better now, which in itself has to be a miracle. But what's happened?"

"I can never return to Aisywel. It no longer exists for me." There was flat finality in her voice.

"What do you mean?"

"I tried to return through a portal but there was only empty space." She looked away, her shoulders slightly hunched. "I can't return."

"God, Pandimora, I'm sorry. Are you sure there isn't another way in?" he said cautiously. Was he buying into this whole faerie realm story? "Irfin claims to be a sorcerer, maybe he can find a way."

"I don't know," she said softly, and the ache in her voice affected him, making him want to protect her.

She pressed her fingertips to her forehead and closed her eyes.

"I don't understand any of this, how this place -- faerie realm even exists," he said. "If it's similar to earth, there's sometimes an alternate way around blockades. Another plan of action. You just have to find the right person to help you figure it out."

She looked like she needed someone to comfort her, hold her close and tell her everything would be okay, but he didn't know that for sure. This entire experience was an unknown to him. He was feeling his way as he went along.

Her hair appeared dry, now down on her shoulders, the heavy braid a flame against the milky skin of her neck. Drew had the notion to stroke the delicate skin, but instead he shoved his hands into his jeans pockets. If she was a faerie, why even think about going there? He had enough trouble understanding human women.

"You look a lot better," he said. "This place really healed you?" Or she was a good actress, but part of him felt a sense of wonder.

"Yes, although the healing is still being integrated. I need a little more time before I will feel once more like myself, then I must work on a plan."

He looked at her sharply. "What plan?"

"I can't give up, but I'm confused and confusion leaves open the possibility for error. When I was a small child and my sister newly born, our family was torn apart. We grew up in the faerie nursery, never knowing something terrible happened to our parents."

"You grew up in an orphanage?"

She hesitated then nodded. "Similar, but for most faeries it is the way of life. Parents go off living their own lives and leave their children to be raised by the wise elders of the faerie realm." She frowned. "I everything I've seen, but it's nothing new that something beautiful can also hide a darkness underneath." He reached for her hand. "Do you think you can leave here and the elder will leave you alone? Look at what he's done to you already," he added tensely. "Let me help you figure this out."

"I can make you go," she said, lips compressed. Her tight grip communicated her distress. Drew looked down, seeing the small blue curls of electricity between their hands.

"I'm sure you can make me go," he said, "but if we work together maybe we can find a solution."

Pandimora looked beyond him into the forest. He watched the trees arch their limbs over them, swaying slightly, as if listening in on their conversation. He narrowed his eyes. Maybe they had to be careful what they said down here too.

He couldn't deny it was a beautiful place, the air filled with a mystical quality he'd never experienced and couldn't even put into words, but no one could live in a fantasy land their entire lives, could they? It would be like existing in a Disney movie.

He didn't want to give her time to cite reasons why he should leave, so he said, "There must be a way I can help you. Maybe we should return to my place and do some research. I'm an investigator after all."

"Right now I don't know how to help myself. I'm struggling to find the truth, and even I might not be who I think I am," she said.

"Maybe that poison is still working on you."

Pandimora shook her head. "I feel very clear headed." Her eyes were almost mesmerizing. "You

∞ Chapter Five ∞

Pandimora studied the rugged planes and sharp angles of Drew's face, his chin with its soft bristle of dark blond stubble, squared and determined. She felt his strong protective instinct that dealt with everyday life on the earth realm. Drew was a man who accomplished much in his world. He wished to help her, but she knew allowing that would endanger him further. She already had mixed feelings about the amount of time they'd spent together. She knew in her heart she was becoming more attracted to him and there could be no happy outcome. She wanted to return to Aisywel and he lived in his world.

"Tell me what you mean," he said now, standing with feet solidly braced in the deep green moss. His deeply muscled chest and shoulders appeared tense. His nose was slightly crooked, and she remembered the day he had broken it while playing football.

Throughout his life she had visited the earth realm to watch him grow and change. And his brown eyes were deep and full of his own secrets, eyes she could get lost in. But she could not. She hadn't been able to stay away, having thought of him often since they were children. Assuming she could return to Aisywel again, she would never leave it forever and he would never be happy there.

"Do you remember that summer your faeries friends came to play? Down by the small creek, in the coolness of the forest?"

He frowned. She knew many times it was difficult for humans to remember themselves as the children they used to be.

The light around them extinguished itself suddenly, as happened in all faerie realms. The light faeries bustled out and about, spraying the air with golden trails of light at their feet.

Shimmering gold flakes touched Drew's shoulders, nestling in his hair, even clinging to his long lashes. Behind him was the faint outline of a portal. All she had to do was walk him toward it. By the time he realized her intent, it would be too late. As much as she enjoyed his company, her world was no place for a human. He could become lost here forever. So lost that even she would not be able to find him.

"We often visited, my sister and me."

He took a step back, staring at her intently, dredging up memories from a time he'd pretty much forgotten. His expression turned to shock. "Pandimora -- yes -- but I forgot about that summer, until this instant. My parents were fighting a lot and only recently learned my father Declan and my mother Clare were different. The elder told me my mother was ill -- she had a madness in her." She shook her head. "The questions go around in my head."

Drew swallowed. "What does that mean?"

"I don't know. He said she had terrible headaches. I've never known anything about my parents."

"You're talking about going up against a powerful elder. Do you have any kind of backup or reinforcements?" At her blank look, he said grimly, "I'll help you however I can."

Her expression turned distant. "You cannot be involved anymore."

Stunned, he said, "Can you do this on your own? One person against an elder with special powers -- or so Irfin claims."

"I have to try," she said fiercely. "But a human would have no defense in our world." She waved her hand at their splendid surroundings. "As beautiful and delightful as this world looks, do not be fooled, it could swallow you up so that you were never found. It's not the first time a human has disappeared into the world of the fae. One wrong step and ..." she shrugged.

That sounded almost too dark and ominous to believe, just as everything here looked too fantastical to believe. Drew, a hard nose about everything, felt himself being sucked into this world. Could it all be true, he wondered?

"Geez, Pandimora, God knows I'm coming around to actually believing in faeries after don't remember me, do you Drew?"

He frowned. "I've felt there was something familiar about you, but to tell the truth I can't place you."

"One summer a long time ago, we played together as children."

∞ Chapter Five ∞

Pandimora studied the rugged planes and sharp angles of Drew's face, his chin with its soft bristle of dark blond stubble, squared and determined. She felt his strong protective instinct that dealt with everyday life on the earth realm. Drew was a man who accomplished much in his world. He wished to help her, but she knew allowing that would endanger him further. She already had mixed feelings about the amount of time they'd spent together. She knew in her heart she was becoming more attracted to him and there could be no happy outcome. She wanted to return to Aisywel and he lived in his world.

"Tell me what you mean," he said now, standing with feet solidly braced in the deep green moss. His deeply muscled chest and shoulders appeared tense. His nose was slightly crooked, and she remembered the day he had broken it while playing football.

Throughout his life she had visited the earth realm to watch him grow and change. And his brown eyes were deep and full of his own secrets, eyes she could get lost in. But she could not. She hadn't been able to stay away, having thought of him often since they were children. Assuming she could return to Aisywel again, she would never leave it forever and he would never be happy there.

"Do you remember that summer your faeries friends came to play? Down by the small creek, in the coolness of the forest?"

He frowned. She knew many times it was difficult for humans to remember themselves as the children they used to be.

The light around them extinguished itself suddenly, as happened in all faerie realms. The light faeries bustled out and about, spraying the air with golden trails of light at their feet.

Shimmering gold flakes touched Drew's shoulders, nestling in his hair, even clinging to his long lashes. Behind him was the faint outline of a portal. All she had to do was walk him toward it. By the time he realized her intent, it would be too late. As much as she enjoyed his company, her world was no place for a human. He could become lost here forever. So lost that even she would not be able to find him.

"We often visited, my sister and me."

He took a step back, staring at her intently, dredging up memories from a time he'd pretty much forgotten. His expression turned to shock. "Pandimora -- yes -- but I forgot about that summer, until this instant. My parents were fighting a lot and on the verge of divorce. That summer, we kids were miserable and a bit lost. When you're young, you don't think about the reality of other worlds. I was about seven. At that age you just accept what you see. But then you stopped coming one day."

She smiled a bit sadly. "Your troubles went away and you grew up. I continued to come but your were older and your eyes were closed to me."

"My parents moved us out west for a time, and then we returned years later."

"I have always been here," she said with a smile. "Even when you no longer saw me." A delicious warmth emanated from his body. Every particle of her being felt the raw energy of his aura. She inhaled his refreshing and intoxicating scent deeply, a scent she would know anywhere.

Captivated by her own dangerously increasing desire to interact with Drew, she cautioned herself, but was still curious as to his heart. Had it healed from his love long ago? It was something she could not look inside, it would be like an invasion of his being. Only he could unlock that part of him so that she might see. And there was no time.

"This is beyond anything I know as an adult," he said. "We go about daily life, never knowing what else might be around us." Drew hesitated. "It's kind of weird, but I always had this interest in ancient worlds and cultures. It fascinated me from when I was a child." He frowned. "Now I'm wondering if even though my childhood memory of your visits faded, there was a still something in me that remembered." He shrugged. "I don't know."

Drew pulled a flashlight from his jacket and

moved it over the area. She realized that for his human eyes, dark had fallen, while she had little difficulty seeing through the shadows around them.

"Our worlds are different Drew, but there are also similarities. We can communicate without words, just as some individuals may do in your world. Everything experienced in this realm is recorded and heard by all."

"Telepathically," Drew said. "What about Irfin?" he asked. "Can we trust him?"

She looked at him, shocked. "Irfin is of importance here as well as in your world."

"Can we trust him?" he repeated. "How can he live in both worlds? What is his real job?"

"He is very clever, having integrated both worlds into his life a long time ago. It can be done, but sometimes it proves to be a difficult transition for the fae. He is not only a sorcerer but also an inventor who created the protective shield for this healing sanctuary."

"He created all this?"

"And much more."

"How long will the shield keep you safe?"

"I believe I can answer that," stated Irfin, his voice above them in the branches of the trees. "It will protect her until its energy is drained, which will depend upon how many times an energy being tries to breach it." Irfin dropped down out of the tree limbs to the ground and smirked at Drew. "I see you fought your way through our industrial strength daisies."

Drew lifted a brow.

"Hmm." Irfin rubbed his bearded chin and

Pandimora saw his green eyes twinkling. "Have you left your sense of humor elsewhere? No matter," Irfin said cheerily, "I have enough humor for a dozen men."

***

Drew studied Irfin's bright eyes, the smirk, knowing it would be a waste of time to be irritated with the man. This was Irfin's world.

So he said, "Just how protected is she if the elder tries to gain access to this place?"

"Each time it will drain the energy a little more. However, anyone trying to see into this dimension must be on the same aura frequency as Pandimora to make the connection. That might take a little more work and mental decoding. The elder has many powers, but even he must work to see into something so intricate as this dimension."

"You seem pretty knowledgeable about such a circumstance. Does that mean Pandimora isn't the first one to be in danger from this elder?"

"Danger to a faerie doesn't have the same meaning as it would to a human. A handful of others relocated outside Aisywel, so we are always prepared for any eventuality. This place was created so those of the fae living in the earth dimension could come here and rejuvenate."

"Like a ... spa?" Drew asked.

Irfin narrowed his eyes. "No. There are no return visits. Faeries are only allowed one visit to rejuvenate. They may come again, but there are never the same results on return visits."

"What about humans? Are they allowed here?"

Irfin turned away. "At times, but the healing

outcome is even less predictable for humans."

"And I'm guessing this sanctuary is operated in secrecy?"

Irfin looked over his shoulder. "That would be one way of looking at it. We saw the need for this sanctuary and it was created long ago, thousands of years in your time. I have simply upgraded it to reflect the changing times." Irfin put his hand out to indicate the glowing world around them. "We are constantly experimenting with the sanctuary. What if we could offer humans the same immortality our race enjoys, if the humans were interested?"

Drew thought Irfin's eyes had a strange, almost feverish glitter. "So that's where you're going?" he said thoughtfully. "Immortality for a select few humans?"

Irfin whipped his head around to glare at him. "I didn't say that."

"I think you did."

"You may draw whatever conclusions you like," Irfin said, bushy brows drawn together.

"Is this sanctuary in some part of Aisywel?"

"No," Pandimora said. "It's a higher dimension since it is a sanctuary. This realm hovers slightly above Aisywel and a little to the side. Elders can penetrate most barriers and worlds; however, there are certain energies which can temporarily block their perception."

"True," added Irfin. "The mechanics of this shield were conceived in the faerie realm but actually created on earth. This intermixing of both worlds has thus far created an impenetrable shield."

"How would a human find their way here?" Drew

asked.

Irfin pulled a yo-yo from his pocket and fiddled with it. "Anyone seeking asylum is welcomed. Mystics and earth healers or those who have become enlightened while incarnating on the earth plane are aware of this place. However, as I mentioned earlier, humans can only gain entrance through one of the fae." His gaze was piercingly on Drew. "Or if you jump a portal while a faerie is transporting."

"I tried to return to Aisywel," Pandimora blurted.

Irfin nodded, his eyes sad. "Was the ground as if turned to vapor?"

"Yes. I was almost pulled into the empty space between dimensions."

"The high elder's duty is to keep the worlds safe and he will do that at any cost," Irfin said grimly. "Right now you are perceived as a threat."

Frustrated, Pandimora said, "If the faerie is found unharmed, then I saw everything wrong." She looked troubled. Drew saw her fingers clench and wondered if she really believed she had been wrong.

Thoughtfully, Irfin said, "The brain has incredible resilience, even more so since the fae utilize twice as much brain matter as a human. I have to wonder about when the elder tried to make you forget what you saw in the garden -- it clearly didn't work. Could it be because you were mind washed as a child? Perhaps a faerie cannot be mind washed twice? It is a question that has intrigued me for years."

"What if half the faeries in Aisywel are walking around with pieces of their reality wiped away?"

Drew said.

"An exaggeration," Irfin declared.

Drew lifted a brow. "But how would you know? And what if a faerie is banished forever and can't return? Has that happened to others?" Drew felt a bit ridiculous asking such a thing, but really, what was off limits anymore?

"You would wander aimlessly, an empty vessel," Pandimora said. "Your heart is empty because Aisywel is the soul of your existence."

Drew stared at her in surprise. "That sounds pretty extreme."

She looked at him. "What if you were exiled by your authority, never to return to the home of your birth, your family -- all that is familiar?"

"It would be difficult for anyone," he agreed.

"I remember being in the faerie nursery and hearing whispers of the wanderers, the soulless ones."

Drew looked at her incredulously. "They told you that kind of stuff when you were little?"

"Little is a relative term," Irfin said. "Faeries remain in the nursery for one hundred and thirty human years. At the end of that time they will in essence resemble a five-year old human child."

Drew was stunned. Pandimora appeared to be in her early twenties. "Does that mean you're over a thousand years old?"

"No," she said, "from about age five to sixteen time moves the same as it does for humans."

"And after sixteen time moves even slower," Irfin said. "We age one year every twenty human years in the faerie world."

Drew pushed his fists into his pockets. "And you never die."

"Faeries are immortal," Irfin agreed, his tone almost somber.

She nodded. "Unless immortality is stolen from us or we choose a life on the earth dimension."

Drew turned to Irfin. "And what about you, Irfin? How old are you?"

"Very, very old," he conceded. "I have seen the changes through the centuries. My father was a pioneer in his day and we gradually grew comfortable living between Aisywel and the earth dimension. Once you are in the fae world, there is always a connection and you are revived back to your roots."

"What happens if you abandon your faerie roots?" he asked.

"Eventually, we would turn mortal. There have been those of the fae who felt the love of a human was worth the cost, and they lived out their lives as mortals."

Drew stared at him, seeing Irfin fidgeting now, sensing some undercurrent about which he could only guess. "How do you play into all this Irfin, besides helping to create this sanctuary?" Drew asked.

"A small group of faeries came to me, knowing of my sorcerer skills. Collectively, we fell upon the idea of creating a buffer between this sanctuary and any elder's frequency. Quite a simple idea, really. I utilize polyphase power, a three-hundred-and-sixty-degree rotating magnetic field that temporarily scrambles an elder's special powers of perception should they look upon this place." He lifted a brow. "We gave the idea to the great physicist Tesla many years ago, but I tweaked it and re-created it for our own use."

"Tesla?" Drew asked. "Are you serious?"

"I worked with him, which was a humbling experience. The man was a genius who sucked up the ideas we gave him and in turn helped give the faerie realm new ideas. There are many times human inspiration comes from the world of the fae and vice versa. Since there have been mini breaches to the magnetic field in recent times, I'm working on a more effective vibrational shield, but it's too unstable to put into place just yet."

Drew studied the other man thoughtfully. "Let's say for the sake of argument this elder is corrupt. With all the power he holds, what more could he want?"

Irfin pulled his yo-yo out of his pocket and let it unspool, then with a smooth lift of his fingers it rolled back up the string toward him. He shrugged. "There is no simple answer. He already controls so much within the dimensions."

Pandimora cleared her throat. "He wants to control everything, eliminate races he feels are unworthy." She shivered. "He will eliminate two thirds of the universe's population. I have heard it whispered there are elders who felt one faerie should not rule for all time. They were in favor of a new high elder every two hundred years."

Drew narrowed his eyes. "So he may have been aware of this sentiment and felt his position was threatened. I imagine it might be difficult to step down from power you've wielded for so long."

Irfin brushed that aside. "Merely speculation. I have heard no talk of dissatisfaction with his rule."

"Until now," Drew said pointedly.

"It was a conversation overheard," Pandimora said. "There may be others who share the same thinking as Drew."

Drew looked at Irfin. "Do you feel the high elder should continue for another thousand years in this position -- especially if he's abusing his power?"

"It sounds like rubbish to me," Irfin said flatly. "There is no concrete proof as yet. I'm done with this discussion." He moved away from them through the trees.

Pandimora watched Irfin with a frown. "I only know what I heard," she said. "The elder told me he asked my mother Clare to come to Aisywel. My mother was human," she ended.

"That must have been a shock for you," he said.

"Any little thing I learn about my parents is a surprise. And yet I know virtually nothing." Pandimora touched her cheek, a faraway look in her eyes. "It makes me sad that I don't remember my parents."

"How do you know he wasn't lying?"

"The crystals don't lie," she said.

"Just remember there's variation on the truth," he said. "It can sometimes be twisted or cut up into pieces and made to look whole again." Drew looked around them. "The more I learn about this place the more I'm filled with amazement. Your father married a human and she adapted to living in Aisywel?"

"Yes."

"Where are your parents?"

"I thought they left my sister and I to travel to a higher dimension, as sometimes happens with faeries that have lived a long time. It is an accepted way of life. But that cannot be since my mother was human. She was not immortal. The elder said my mother ran off one night. No one had ever spoken to myself or my sister of my parents."

Irfin walked back toward them, a clay smoking pipe clenched in one hand. He put his hands behind his back and braced his feet wide. "There are faeries that live solely in the earth realm." He sighed, no doubt seeing their confusion. "They have been left alone to live there and have families. Many have forgotten they are of the fae. Many thousands of years ago, all faerie lived together, alongside the elves, leprechauns and the sprites in Aisywel. We all are aware of each race, but occupy our own space. There was also a time when humans and faeries dwelled together, but as sometimes happens there were power struggles over land and space, and we became the hidden people."

"There really are elves?" Drew asked.

"And brownies, the knockers, the bogeyman -- ones of which the humans have told frightening tales to their children for many a year," Irfin conceded. "Those are the mischievous ones. They are part and parcel of the fae world, but in truth I don't like to acknowledge their bad behavior visited upon the humans."

"And I never thought faerie tales were anything other than stories," Drew muttered.

"They are true enough. Any story ever told has

some basis in reality."

Pandimora fretted. "And another reality is that I cannot stay in this lovely healing sanctuary. The elder is searching for me, and anywhere I remain will be put at risk the longer I stay. I must leave."

Irfin looked at her. "I must agree, although I will try to mask you as best I can," he said. "I have a small experimental shield you can carry on your person. It may offer protection, but until I perfect the larger shield, everyone here is in danger ..." his voice trailed off.

"I don't like it," Drew said. "Too much is stacked in his favor. What about those power crystals? How do you fight against those? Is there any way to disarm them?"

Both Irfin and Pandimora looked at him, aghast. "It is not advised to alter the crystals," said Irfin. "The outcome could be unpredictable for all life."

"Right at this moment I can't wrap my head around faeries, much less ego driven ones," he said.

"Humans have the wrong impression about our race," Irfin said. "We are not vengeful. We pretty much just want to keep to ourselves. Long ago the ancient ones saw the need for protection against the immense upheaval in the world's climate that gave rise to cataclysmic events across all dimensions. The crystals were created from precious stone specimens which appeared to hold an energy force within their structure. They became a powerful foundation of balance for all worlds. If the crystal's power is disrupted, the dark creatures below could once more roam all worlds, even the earth dimension. Unrest would ensue, manifesting itself in unpredictable weather patterns."

"Like we don't have unpredictable weather already?" Drew asked.

"You have no idea the scope of what could occur," Irfin cautioned. "The earth could crack apart like an egg."

"It's mind boggling, all this going on under the surface," Drew remarked, frowning. Could Irfin be telling the truth?

"The crystals keep the realms stable, and all dimensions go about their daily life as they expect it to be. In ancient times one of the crystals disappeared, which divided the faerie realms. Long ago the dark creatures existed alongside Aisywel faeries, but when the crystal disappeared suspicion turned to them and they were not allowed above ground again."

"What dark creatures?" asked Drew. "There's others?"

"The Deevs occupy the lowest dimension of all worlds. It is said they stole the third crystal, but no proof has ever been found to support such a theory." He looked at Pandimora. "If we had the third crystal, you could find all the truths. I have searched through time, but I have had no success. It is prophesized the crystal will resurface when the time is right but surprisingly little else is known."

Pandimora's eyes grew wide. Drew looked at Irfin. "But if the Deevs have it wouldn't they be able to free themselves, if it has some kind of power?"

"There is no answer," Irfin said soberly. "The crystals have varying powers, but finding the third crystal would enable someone to stand on equal footing with the elder."

Drew saw the expression on Pandimora's face. His shoulders tensed. "You can't be thinking of trying to find the missing crystal, Pandimora? It sounds --"

"Dangerous?" she asked, nodding. "Possibly. But the risk would be worth it. Right now I am exiled from my home, without my sister and I have no answers about a family that disappeared long ago." She frowned. "What do I have to lose?"

"Your life," he said grimly.

"And what is life without the ones held deeply within your heart?"

Drew had a sinking feeling about this whole thing. "If a sorcerer couldn't find the crystal, what could you do that he hasn't done already?"

"I have a gift," she said, now looking stubborn, her eyes flashing. "To find that which is hidden."

Drew looked at Irfin. "You started this. What do you think?"

Irfin gave Pandimora a speculative glance. "It may take someone with a special gift to find the crystal." He shrugged. "I will not deny it will be dangerous. I imagine the elder also searches."

"How did this elder come into all this power?" Drew wondered aloud.

"Lukais came into power when Declan, the high lord of the faeries, disappeared." Irfin looked at Pandimora. "Your father and the high elder were friends. The night Clare and Declan disappeared the high elder stepped into his place to calm the chaos that ensued. Eventually, he was entrusted also with the care of the crystals, combining both responsibilities into one."

Drew looked at Irfin. "And how do you know all this?"

"I lived it," Irfin said.

"Can you tell me anything about my parents?" Pandimora asked. Drew heard the wistful note in her voice and hoped anything Irfin told her could ease some of the devastation she must be feeling.

However, Irfin's expression became troubled. "Declan, Clare and Kirklas disappeared the same night --"

Pandimora looked stunned. "Who is Kirklas?"

"Your brother -- half brother."

She began to breathe hard, her eyes wide. "Why can't I remember?"

Calmly, Irfin continued. "Kirklas was Declan's first born. It was said your father found the waif when his mother died."

Drew stared at Irfin. Could this get any more complicated? Now she found out she had a brother. "His mother died?"

"I don't actually know for sure. There seemed to be an element of secrecy about the appearance of Kirklas, but Declan claimed the child as his own. In truth, when Kirklas arrived, he had light brown hair and blue eyes. When a young child comes into a fae household, they begin to identify and look like the elder of the household. Kirklas grew to look like Declan. Dark hair, bright green eyes. He was fully accepted as Declan's son. He was about four earth years when Declan brought him home, still several years before he met Clare."

"Where did he find Kirklas?" Drew asked.

"It was said Kirklas is part human, part faerie."

A shiver snaked up Drew's neck. "Could he have been stolen?"

"No!" Irfin said adamantly, giving Drew an annoyed stare. "No. Declan was an honorable man, high lord of the faeries." Irfin turned his attention to Pandimora and continued. "When Clare came to Aisywel she was ill, suffering terrible pain in the head. It was said Declan saw her and instantly fell in love and until they disappeared he loved Clare endlessly and beyond. Clare loved Kirklas as her own, but when they all disappeared, there seemed to be no answers found."

"Was this a normal occurrence back then?" Drew said, watching Pandimora grapple with all she'd learned.

"No."

"Because my mother was human?" Pandimora whispered.

"Because she was a white witch. I recall thinking it was a strange circumstance to have a human living in Aisywel, but Clare adapted and all faerie children seemed to love her. She never turned away a child that showed up on the doorstep. Many a night a faerie child would be in front of the fire or gobbling down one of her fine stews in the kitchen."

Irfin pulled the small pipe from his shirt pocket and tapped it against his knee. "After Declan, Kirklas is the rightful high lord of the faeries. But again, there is no knowledge of Kirklas' whereabouts, and we may never know." His words chilled Drew. There seemed to be a hint of troubling detachment in Irfin's words. He had to wonder if he knew more than he was letting on.

The little man turned to Pandimora. "Only you can prove the reality of what you experienced. Did the elder strike down another faerie or was there something else going on, something you didn't understand?"

"I know what I saw," she said stubbornly.

Irfin stared at his pipe. "Just be sure," he cautioned. "Accusations made must be accurate and not a misinterpretation on your part. If it is all true, then there will assuredly be an interrogation by the high elder council."

"And if Pandimora's memory is faulty?" Drew asked.

"Pandimora will be forever stricken from faerie memory," Irfin said soberly.

Drew heard her indrawn breath, saw the devastation on her face. He wondered if it was like being branded a traitor in his world.

"Do you know anything more about her family's disappearance?" Drew asked.

Irfin hesitated, but relented upon seeing the pleading look on Pandimora's face. "There was talk Clare may have run off due to the mental illness she suffered," he said reluctantly. "Unfortunately, that's all I know. I did a lot of traveling back then. I was more interested in traveling through various dimensions than staying in Aisywel where each day is the same. I'm sorry I can tell you no more."

Drew thought of Deborah, who'd been bi-polar and suffered from anxiety and delusions. He thought of his own guilt over the tragic circumstances of her death. Ghosts hung around a long time; he'd been trying to exorcise Deborah's for more than five years. He had to wonder if Pandimora's mother suffered from a similar illness?

"I must find the truth about my family." Pandimora crossed her arms, her mouth set. "My gift is to find that which is lost or hidden." She nodded decisively. "I cannot give up."

∞ Chapter Six ∞

Pandimora lay still on the soft ferns, the green fronds tickling her. She blew at one by her nose, touching a fingertip to the soft fronds. The life force of the fern pulsed between her fingertips, then she gently pressed it down to her bed.

So bravely and with assurance she had spoken earlier. She would find the truth about her family.

In the quiet of the evening she chastised herself. Who was she to make such a claim? A half-human faerie thrust from her home. She couldn't even find her own sister. And now to learn she also had a brother. Her heart ached with heaviness. If she found the powerful missing crystal, could she then know the truth of her family?

"Pandimora." Drew.

She rolled onto her back, staring up at him in the dim light. How caring his human heart, and even now his concern enfolded her. But this was her mission, her responsibility.

He knelt beside her in the ferns and she loved having him so close. His jacket lay beside him. No doubt his body had adjusted to the perfectly controlled atmosphere around them.

She reached out and traced the curve of his cheek with her finger. Such a determined and brave man. She lay the back of her fingers along his jaw. She enjoyed touching Drew very much and that in and of itself could create complications. Eventually, he would return to his world and she to hers.

"I lay here wondering how I'll find out about my family," she admitted. "I don't even know where to start. I wonder that I spoke such brave words with nothing to back them up."

His fingers splayed along the ground on either side of him as he balanced on the balls of his feet. "You said it's your gift? Can you explain?"

Pandimora propped herself up on an elbow. "Every faerie is born with a gift that is intrinsic to their soul. The gift is usually identified before what you would consider a child's tenth birth year. My sister has the gift of healing, while my gift is to find that which is lost. But in truth I have never actually used this gift, except in ways that were trivial."

"It's a lifelong gift?" he asked.

She nodded.

"Tell me about it," he said encouragingly.

Pandimora lay back. "There was a time a ball sank to the bottom of the lake, and everyone saw it thrown into the water. Surely an easy find for a faerie, even without her soul gift?

"On another occasion little Maveen, playing a

game of hide and seek, hid behind a barrel of the sweetest pickles made in all of Aisywel." She smiled. "I had quite a fondness for the pickles and discovered her hiding spot when I reached in the barrel to grab a delicious pickle.

"The first time my soul gift was identified was the day I'd found the beautiful colored chalks the nursery marm had hidden high upon a shelf. All sparkly and bright, they called to me from across the faerie nursery. They were supposed to be a treat for some later activity, but when the nursery marm returned to the nursery with her cup of tea, I was decorating my arms and legs with the various colors."

"Even if you haven't used your gift often, it sounds important." She felt his faith in her down to her toes. "All faeries have a unique gift?"

"Of course. Some faeries see to the growth of all plant life. Then others watch the clouds in the sky and help form them into shapes. Others create the glorious colors in fall leaves. Faeries are instrumental in overseeing everyday life most humans take for granted."

"I had no idea." Drew was amazed at the scope of responsibilities faeries seemed to have, not only for their own world, but the earth. "This is all just so incredible," he said. "So much so that it seems like a dream."

"The scent of flowers are woven by faerie magic. The touch of the wind on your cheek is sweet faerie breath. The world of the fae has always been charmed by magic." Her voice deepened in distress. "In Aisywel, all faeries comport themselves in a certain manner, but I am different."

"I don't know about faeries," he said, a half smile framing his lips. "But it can be difficult for anyone who's an individual and therefore seen as different."

"While I've always taken comfort in Aisywel's safe predictability, that is now gone. I feel --" she hesitated, loss a heavy weight upon her breast.

"Lost?" he asked, compassion in his voice.

She nodded. "I have no home, no safe haven." Pandimora moved to sit with her arms around her up-drawn legs and pressed her forehead to her knees. "How can I find the truth if I can never return home?"

"Maybe this is only temporary and eventually you will return," he said. "You're strong, Pandimora and determined."

"I don't feel strong," she muttered against her knees.

"Do you have a plan?"

Pandimora looked back toward the glen where the trail of fireflies glowed like ripe gold strands.

"I will leave here," she said. "And you will go back to your own life."

His head went back. "I thought we sorted this out. I'm coming with you."

She pressed her chin down harder to her knees. "This is something I have to do alone."

"So you're going to disappear, just like that?" he said. She could hear the anger in his voice.

"There is no other option," Pandimora said, stiffening her resolve. She wanted nothing more than to allow Drew to stay with her, but she knew it was a dangerous and selfish desire.

She rose and stretched, tensing and relaxing her muscles, making sure all residues of pain had been eliminated. Gently, she rubbed her fingers over the mark on her arm.

"That tattoo is back to normal," he said, pointing at the star's outline.

"Not really. Until all this occurred, the star had eight points. Now it has twelve. I had always wondered how it came to be. The crystal hologram showed our mother marked my sister and I. The faerie at the healing sanctuary said it was for protection, but there are so many questions."

"At least tell me where you plan to start your search?"

"There are many possibilities -- other realms."

"I can help you find your sister. That's what I do, Pandimora."

"I will accept your help, Drew, if indeed the search leads me to your world."

"How will I know if you're all right?"

She pressed her palm lightly to his lean cheek, seeing small thin sparks jump between them. "Such sweet concern, but all connection must be severed. I cannot take a chance and have you come to the elder's attention. I must go back into our family history. If I can discover a trace of Kirklas, perhaps I can discover if he is still immortal." She frowned. "I can't think of anything else but finding my family. It consumes me."

"That's understandable," he said. "I don't know if you're incredibly brave or incredibly foolish to attempt this on your own. I want you to survive this," he added fiercely.

Pandimora leaned close, placed her arms around him and pressed a soft kiss to his neck. Surely she could take this little bit of remembrance with her? Being close to Drew. Yearning swept through her and she felt a similar desire rise in him. Somehow their relationship had subtly shifted. Their worlds were so different, and yet she felt increasingly drawn to him. Her heart ached for the loss of a family she had never had the chance to grieve, and it also ached because she must send Drew away. Their worlds were too different. But then a small voice whispered, you are part human.

Pandimora wondered if this would be the last time she would see him. Drew bent down and placed a kiss on her lips and she sank deeply into the kiss for several moments, their contact instantly inflaming her. His scent was intoxicating. She brushed her hand through his hair, her fingertips tracing his ears and the back of his scalp. Heat began to build and blue light snapped between their bodies. Slowly, and with regret, she pulled away until they stood very close but no longer touching. She could still feel the energy from his body embracing her.

"Goodbye, Drew," she said softly, and she pushed him firmly backward into the portal she had manifested.

***

"Pandimora! Damn it!" Drew yelled. But only the hills and distant mountains heard him as he landed on his feet in the road. He caught his balance before he fell to the snowy ground, then turned full circle on his heel. He looked through the blowing snow. He was back at Dell's Bridge and his truck was gone.

"No!" He turned around, cupping his eyes to protect them from the snow. "No! My truck -- could anything else be messed up tonight?" It was approximately ten miles back to town and with the new interstate, traffic through this area was pretty sparse.

Drew looked at his watch, something he hadn't thought to do once while in that other place. Six o'clock. The evening air was crisp and cold. Barely twenty four hours had passed since Pandimora fell into the road in front of him, but he felt as if his entire life and everything he thought he'd known about the world had spun a dizzying three-hundred-and-sixty degrees. Faeries, leprechauns and elves. Holy crap, how could he reconcile their existence in his mind?

And Pandimora. He took a deep breath. Yes, Pandimora. Just thinking about her made his adrenalin speed up. Sweet, strong, with hair as red as fire. She and Irfin were from a world as far removed from his own as could be, but what else might be hidden he didn't know about? And now he would freeze to death if he didn't start hoofing it back to town.

Drew looked at his cell phone again, then shoved it back into his pocket. It appeared to be dead. He began walking. He hadn't gone a hundred yards when he knew this would be a grueling walk.

His T-shirt was poor protection against the flurries and cold of the impending night. No doubt his heavy jacket was back in the sanctuary somewhere. He had a small pen light, but who knew how long that would last? Just as that thought crossed his mind, the sky fully clouded over and snow began to fall even faster.

He eyed the black clouds moving in over the mountains and began jogging up the middle of the road. If he was lucky, he'd make it to town in a few hours, an hour and a half if he really pushed it.

He'd only jogged a few miles when he heard an approaching vehicle. The snow coating his shoulders had also found its way down his neck and he'd been trying to ignore the chill of his wet cotton T-shirt.

The car slowed and he turned to see a small Smart car, green with black trim. It pulled up beside him and the darkened passenger window moved down.

"Like a lift?" asked a familiar voice.

Drew looked inside the open window. "Yes!" he said with relief. He reached for the handle and opened the door, then got inside and pulled the door closed. "Am I glad to see you, Irfin."

Irfin frowned, his thick brows rising. In the dim interior of the car his brows and hair actually looked darker. "Sorry, you've mistaken me for someone else. Glad to give you a ride though." Irfin reached forward and turned the heat dial all the way up.

"You don't know me?" Drew asked sarcastically, which earned him a look of surprise. He put his head back against the head rest. "Never mind. Thanks for stopping. Nice car," he added with a short laugh. "I bet it's great on gas."

"It gets me where I need to go," Irfin said, eyeing him warily.

"You look like him," Drew muttered. "Except for

the hair." He shook his head, feeling exhausted as the sudden heat of the car enveloped him. "I just spent all night hanging out with you and Pandimora."

"Sorry, I don't know you," the man who looked and sounded like Irfin said, peering through the windshield as the flakes increased in intensity.

Drew stared at him. "Aren't you a sorcerer?"

The man smiled. "I was a magician once in a magic show. What are you doing walking in the middle of nowhere with a storm brewing?"

"Long story." Drew settled back against the surprisingly comfortable seat. He wondered where Pandimora might be right now.

"You look a bit glum," said the man.

Drew looked over at him. This was his opportunity to find out more about Irfin, if he was Irfin. "I've just been thrown out by a woman who thinks she doesn't need my help."

"Women can be independent creatures," observed the other man.

"Tell me about it." Drew said. "That sounds like the voice of experience. You married?"

The other man's face softened for a moment. "Many years. Sometimes though, no matter how long you've been together, it's still not enough." He shot Drew a glance. "You?"

Drew looked out the snow covered window. "No."

"Sorry to hear that. It must be lonely without a mate," the man observed.

Drew made a non-committal sound. Life with Deborah had been unpredictable. Part of him felt guilty that he didn't miss it. "When we get to town you can just drop me off anywhere." He pulled out his phone. He needed to get it charged so he could see if Sara was able to take over his meeting with Mary Palmer. He frowned at the phone. It wasn't dead after all. "The date's messed up on my phone." He set the date back. "Never had that happen before."

"Time moves in crazy fashion, don't you think?" the Irfin look-alike said, his voice almost whimsical. "Everything in life is marked by minutes and hours of the day."

"What did you say your name was?"

"I didn't."

He waited expectantly, but the man offered nothing further. "Do you have a brother named Irfin?"

The man shook his head. "No."

They rode the rest of the way in silence. When they finally rode into town, they passed the sheriff's office, the windows surprisingly dark. The car slowed, then pulled to the curb. Across the street were his investigative offices.

"How did you know where to stop?" Drew asked, looking at the man.

"You said the middle of town."

Drew hadn't said any such thing, but could see he wasn't getting anything out of him. "Thanks again. I really appreciate the ride, Irfin."

"Glad I came along."

Drew opened his door. As he was climbing out, his knee hit the glove compartment and the small compartment door popped open. Inside were half a dozen various colored yo-yo's. He looked up at the driver but the car was already moving ahead, the door closing on its own.

Drew hunched his shoulders as the cold flakes drifted down his neck again, staring after the car. Its rear lights faded into the snowy night. Why had Irfin denied knowing him? Was he protecting himself? Drew gave up trying to figure things out right now. At least he'd been saved from a freezing walk.

First thing in the morning he needed to find out if his truck had been towed to the impound lot. You'd think they'd have cut him some slack before towing it. It's not like that highway was busy, especially this time of year. And anyone in town would have known it was his vehicle. If nothing else the registration in the glove box would give them a clue. He supposed with the storm, everything was closed except for emergencies. It certainly didn't warrant an emergency call to get the sheriff out of bed tonight.

He stood looking up and down the quiet street, and as he did so a familiar itch tickled the back of his neck. He'd done enough surveillance himself to know when he was under observation, but the street was empty even of cars. Drew stared at the front of his brick faced office as he crossed the street. Everything looked the same but something felt off.

Drew grabbed the spare key in a magnetic box under the mailbox and let himself inside the heavy glass security door of the professional office building.

He stomped his feet on the large mat, then strode

down the short hallway to his office, flipping on the hallway light. He paused a moment in disbelief. The glass display case on the wall was broken, glass everywhere. "Not my swords!" He'd collected ancient weaponry the last eight years. Most of his collection was at his house, but he'd displayed two ancient swords here in the office. "I don't believe this!" One of the Celtic swords was missing. The two had been a set and now one was gone.

More than annoyed, Drew knew there was a small chance of getting it back. Stuff like that could disappear underground and never resurface in his lifetime. He'd still file a report, but he wasn't holding out much hope. Drew studied the break and the way the glass still rested on the wood above the bottom sword. Even the wood had been damaged, as if someone had punched or used a blunt object to break the case open.

Drew strode to his desk, reaching the phone and hitting speed dial for his answering service. He was surprised to find six new messages. Usually his business partner Sara retrieved messages when he was out of the office and he did the same for her. Drew plugged his cell into its charger, sitting on the edge of the large wooden desk. He looked back at the hallway, at the empty space where his sword should have been.

"Drew," his brother Grey's voice came across the line, "Work called to tell me they towed your truck. I've left messages all over -- where are you? Mom and Dad are worried. Give me a call and tell me what's going on."

"Are you serious?" he muttered. "I've been gone

twenty hours."

The next message was his mother's voice. Her voice was calm but he could hear the underlying concern. She asked him to call right away. There was another call from the dispatcher at the sheriff's department who had towed his truck and one from his partner Sara. She sounded out of breath and just briefly said she was sorry for spending so much time away from the office but she'd meet up with him tomorrow to discuss their cases. "Good idea," he said to himself. Sara had been spending a lot of time volunteering at the sheriff's department. He'd wanted to talk to her about it because a few of their cases were falling behind schedule. The last call was again from his brother.

"The world's gone crazy," he muttered, disconnecting his brother's call. "You'd think I was gone missing."

He pulled his wet shirt over his head and froze as the muted glow from the streetlights shining into the office window showed someone standing in the shadows across the room. It's times like this he wished he still carried a pistol.

The air in his office suddenly became oppressive, hitting Drew in the chest. Dropping his soggy shirt, he tried to find the wall switch behind him.

"Who's there?" he said warily.

"Where is Pandimora?"

Tension squeezed through Drew, even while the pressure increased in his chest. Was he suffering a heart attack? "I don't know."

"I believe you do know. She is ill and needs attention."

"This is my place and I want you to leave."

He was suddenly propelled backward, along the wall, through the doorway and into the hall, his boots barely touching the wood floor. Drew's back hit the wood paneling with a thud, rattling the broken display rack on the wall above him. He closed his eyes a moment and gritted his teeth, hoping the remaining sword didn't come down and lop off his head.

"Where is she?" the voice boomed all around him, but he still couldn't see anyone.

"I don't know."

"Such loyalty to a faerie you just met. Is she worth your human life?" The voice deepened and Drew suppressed a sense of foreboding. Reaching up, he fumbled with the rack and closed his hand around the remaining Celtic sword. He pulled it down, gripped the double-swirled hilt with both hands, and took a wide stance, swinging the thick sword in a wide arc. He hit something soft and an electric current traveled into his hands, up his arms and into his chest. He dropped the blade and it clattered to the floor. He weaved on his feet, suddenly disoriented.

"Do not meddle in what you don't understand." The voice sounded distorted and further away.

Drew couldn't answer. He had trouble breathing with the weight in his chest and a terrible dizziness in his head. He dropped to one knee.

Vaguely, he was aware of a cold draft. The outer door, which should have automatically locked when he came in earlier, was open. He struggled back to his feet.

"Drew?"

Drew leaned against the wall and looked over his shoulder, adrenaline starting to pump. "Irfin!"

The little man hurried to him. He now wore a puffy black winter jacket, and looked all but lost inside the material.

Drew regained his feet, his hand on the wall for balance, then he turned on the overhead lights, having no trouble now finding the switch. He blinked in the stark brightness and looked around.

"What are you looking for?" Irfin asked, clearly puzzled.

Drew shot him a look. "The elder was here."

Irfin's eyes widened with alarm. "What are you talking about?"

"He was here. And why are you back?" he said. "You give me a ride and pretend not to know me." Drew dropped into a plush hallway chair. He put his head back against the wall, waiting for his heart to stop racing.

"I've known you since I met you, Drew." Irfin's glance settled on the sword on the floor. He went down on one knee. "This is surely a prize," he said, reverently touching the sword with its nicked blade. "And you've drawn blood."

Drew looked down. "Not mine, his." He had the satisfaction of seeing the color leave Irfin's face.

"Oh, now he will be angry, very angry. Not good," Irfin said heavily. "Tell me everything that happened."

Drew did so. "When I swung the blade, it felt like it slowed down as it went through something. Everything around me seemed to shift and I got a

God almighty shock through the metal so I dropped it. The pain in my chest felt like I was having a heart attack."

Irfin rubbed his short beard, the scratching sound of the coarse hair amplified to Drew's ears. "If you managed to penetrate his energy, he may have suffered a loss of resonance -- rather strange since he'd know the earth realm is of a heavier density and to avoid contact with you." His glance settled once more on the sword and his eyes narrowed. "This Celtic sword was once a prized possession taken into battle. The true answer to its power may lie in its ancient origins." He traced a finger over the triskele swirls on the hilt. "The bronze may have acted as a conductor and allowed an exchange of energy." Irfin looked at him, then down at his feet. "You're lucky you had on rubber-soled boots."

"I feel lucky to be alive," Drew muttered. "So in future don't get into his aura. Could I have wounded him enough to incapacitate him?" he asked hopefully.

Irfin snorted, rolling his eyes. "Hardly." But watching him, Drew thought he detected a hint of uncertainty. "It was a momentary aberration," Irfin said dismissively. "He will be on guard next time."

Drew groaned. "Next time? If he's so powerful, how did I catch him unawares?"

Irfin shrugged. "Perhaps he underestimated you or perhaps there is a residue of power left in this blade. Or maybe it was merely luck. After all, you're only human."

"You know Irfin, your sense of humor sucks."

Irfin peered closely at the double-swirled hilt,

then placed the sword on a small side table. "I have a small device that will boost any protection this sword already gives. It may fit nicely between the swirls of the hilt. I'll see to it," he added.

"I should get it to a lab for testing," Drew muttered, staring at the splotches of blood along the blade.

Irfin drew out a white handkerchief and calmly wiped the blade. "You can have it tested all you like. It will yield only limited answers." He calmly refolded the handkerchief and placed it back in his pants pocket.

Drew rolled his head back on his neck to ease some of the tension in his shoulders. He was starting to feel normal again, thank God. "So why don't you save me time and tell me what the test results will show since you're just destroyed the evidence?"

"There will be traces of human DNA with some anomalies. Data may well indicate a hybrid species; males of an unknown hominid species crossing with female Homo sapiens."

"Human females mixing with non-human males?"

"Simply put, yes. Somewhere along time."

"So does this go back to stories of human infants being switched with faerie infants?"

Irfin sighed. "In your medieval times and before, yes, this happened upon occasion when an infusion of new blood was needed by the fae. It was all by prior arrangement. It's not like there were stolen children."

Drew stared at Irfin, incredulous. "Well, that's a different take. How was it arranged?"

"In the dreaming state."

"Sounds sketchy. All kinds of weird stuff happens in dreams."

"Dreaming is where humans are allowed to lift out of their heavy earth body and visit other worlds. Switching infants in present times is forbidden."

"As far as you know," Drew said grimly.

"It is forbidden," Irfin said emphatically, his green eyes flashing. "It is stepping beyond the bounds of today's rules of the fae. We are more in tune with these times. Just as you progress, so do we."

"Well, I'm going to reserve judgment on babies being switched, especially since you mentioned Pandimora's brother Kirklas may have been part human."

"Look at it this way, Drew. That was a long time ago. No doubt Declan pulled him from a miserable existence."

"Yeah, and now he's missing," Drew said.

Irfin sighed. "Point taken."

"Well, with elders having secret agendas, it makes me wonder what else could be going on that no one knows about. Maybe child snatching is still prevalent."

Irfin shook his head. "No. All faeries would know if something like that was happening."

Drew felt tired right out. That interaction really knocked him for a loop. "Hang on a minute. Let me get a dry shirt in my office." Drew walked back into his office, stretching gingerly. His back felt a bit achy from being slammed into the wood. He leaned down and opened the bottom drawer of his desk, pulling out a neatly folded, long-sleeved t-shirt. As he pulled it over his head he noticed a manila envelope on his desk. The return address was Mary Palmer. He opened the envelope and shook the contents onto his desk. He stared down at a picture, then pushed it aside to look at the one underneath.

"So faeries would know if there was child switching going on," Drew murmured. He closed the envelope and carried it to the door. He looked at Irfin. "That's comforting to know -- Rick."

The man's eyes barely flickered.

Drew stared at him hard. "That is your name, right? Rick Palmer, married to Mary Palmer."

For once the other man wasn't cracking jokes.

"Rick -- Irfin, which is it?" Drew asked, pulling out a glossy five-by-six picture and holding it up. "I knew you looked different in the car, though it was hard to tell with the lighting that you had gray hair. Suitable, I guess, if you're married to an eighty-something-year-old human you'd want to look the part. Being a sorcerer, the transformation probably isn't hard to pull off. You lied about who you are. What else have you lied about?"

"Mary knows me as Rick," the other man acknowledged.

"Does she know you're a leprechaun and that you're immortal?"

He nodded.

Drew frowned, letting the picture drop back onto the desk. "Then why would she hire me to find you?"

Irfin sighed. "If you've met with my Mary, then you know she is very ill. We've been together a long time, Mary and I. She's the reason I got involved in the healing sanctuary."

Drew snapped his fingers. "You were trying to make her better, stop her aging. Maybe you even hoped for immortality for her," he said.

Irfin nodded, his eyes immeasurably sad. "Yes. Long ago when the illness first came upon her, I took her to the sanctuary and it helped to some degree, but not as I had hoped. Sometimes that happens."

"So why hire me at a substantial fee to track you down? It sounds like all she wants is for you to come home."

"You're right, but while there's hope for her to be cured and reverse her aging, I can't do that. I have to try and finish what I've started, though at times I've been tempted to give it all up."

"What is it you're involved in?" Drew asked. But now Irfin remained stubbornly silent. When it became clear he wasn't saying anything more, Drew tried another tack. "Are you in league with the elder?"

"There are some things a human wouldn't understand. I have to do what I have to do and that's all I can say." Abruptly, he thrust his hand toward Drew. In his palm was a silver disc about the size of a pocket watch. "This is experimental and may offer you limited protection. Pandimora has a similar device."

Drew didn't take it. "How did the elder find me?"

Irfin shrugged. "Traces of your body chemistry no doubt intermixed with Pandimora's faerie scent from the moment you touched her. It would be easy enough to find you."

"Or someone tipped him off." Drew stared at

Irfin. "The game is set in your world's favor and humans are shoved around like chess pieces."

"You have more power than you think. Look how you pierced the elder's aura. I am amazed you were able to do so. I imagine he is also."

Drew watched as the man adjusted tiny knobs on the side of the silver device. The silver casing had gold discs inside a domed glass which continuously rotated and moved across each other. The discs themselves were etched with blue increments.

Drew looked at it warily. "What do I have to know about this?"

"Nothing. There," Irfin said with satisfaction. "I've calibrated it to your denser specs."

Gingerly, Drew accepted the device, holding it between his thumb and forefinger. It was heavier than it looked.

"It will help."

"That remains to be seen," Drew muttered, unconvinced.

"If humans were more open to innovation, your world would be more advanced when it comes to the use of energy." Irfin moved to the front window and stared out onto the street. "You know he'll be back, right?"

"It did occur to me," Drew said. "So did you send him here?"

Irfin stared at him in surprise. "No."

"Why should I believe you? I think you're hiding something."

"We all hide things," Irfin acknowledged. "Even you, Drew."

"Me?" Drew shrugged, dropping the device in his

pocket. "I'm an open book."

"More like a book with pages torn out."

"Funny."

"Like many humans, you avoid the issues of your own life. Have you ever dealt with your wife's untimely death?"

Drew tensed.

"Humans can have gigantic egos." Irfin put up a hand. "Now I'm not saying that's the case in your life, but really, when is a human ever responsible for someone else's actions and thoughts?"

"You don't know anything about it," Drew said irritably. "Mind your own business."

Irfin continued anyway. "Let me just say the fae see events and even emotions in black and white. We don't get as heavily involved in that aspect of life as do humans. A situation is what it is. If we don't like it, we move on and around it."

"Pandimora's not like that, otherwise she wouldn't be hurt and searching for her family."

"That's because she's part human."

"What's your point?"

"You're only responsible for your own self and your own life."

"I get it," Drew snapped. "But as you said, you see it in black and white. Until I'm able to do that, I'll go on as before."

"Stuck."

"Listen, you're avoiding the issue. Are you hiding something that might in turn harm Pandimora?"

"Don't worry about Pandimora now. You're out of her life," Irfin said. "Your interactions were nothing more than a dream." He lifted a brow.

"Unless you're wanting more? I wouldn't recommend it, faerie and human. Many times it ends up badly."

"And you would know," Drew growled, annoyed by Irfin's interference. "Are you feeding Lukais information that may harm Pandimora?"

"No."

"But you have an association with him."

"None of that concerns you."

"I think it all spills over," Drew said. He stared at the dark street outside and the storm that raged. Where was Pandimora?

"It is unfortunate you have been involved in this business of faeries," Irfin mused. "However, with your background, I think you are better prepared than most."

"With humans, maybe. I'm not so sure about your world."

"You have a built-in preparedness for dangerous situations. It's quite interesting. Human coincidence never ceases to amaze me."

"How do you know this isn't all planned?" The notion had occurred to Drew on his walk back from Dell's Bridge. "Maybe we're all being manipulated. Even you."

Irfin dismissed that with a shake of his head. "In the world of the fae we create absolute outcomes. It's humans who convolute time and circumstance, making end results unpredictable."

"So you're saying everything that's happened since I met Pandimora last night is all a coincidence?"

Irfin grinned. "Seven days have passed here

since you entered the healing sanctuary."

Drew felt pole axed. "No wonder my family has been frantic to reach me."

"For human convenience, time was adopted by your race aeons ago and perceived as a linear line of events, and therefore it moves faster here than in the world of the fae. In the reality of the universe, all time happens simultaneously."

"If that were true, Pandimora would have already reached a conclusion about her family and what occurred in Aisywel. She wouldn't have to go searching for clues."

"True."

"So why let her go through with all this?"

"Because each entity, whether human, fae or otherwise, has to see and understand the end result of their endeavors for their own satisfaction. Even for the fae, things can sometimes remain murky and out of sight. Pandimora must experience and feel the outcome of her own investigation."

"Is the elder hunting Pandimora to keep her safe or does he plan to harm her?"

"The truth of that will come," Irfin said evasively.

"That's it?" Drew asked, disgruntled with such an insufficient answer.

"Pandimora is well aware of the risk in pursuing the truth. There will be no swaying her until she finds her family and the truth about what happened in Aisywel."

"Why come here tonight?"

"When I wound back time I realized I gave you a ride into town when Pandimora kicked you out of the healing sanctuary. I could not let us part on such terms."

"She didn't kick me out."

"You're not there with her." Irfin smirked.

"What do you mean you wound back time?"

"When I gave you a ride, I hadn't met you yet."

"We met at the sanctuary!"

Irfin shook his head. "Before I entered the healing sanctuary I wound back my earth watch to account for the time differences between the two realms. I knew if I did not move back time I would be late for an appointment tomorrow, which is actually today. However, I overcompensated and moved time back too much."

Drew just stared at him. "That's confusing and makes no sense."

"I'm explaining why I did not recognize you when I offered you a ride."

"Where is Pandimora now?"

Irfin fidgeted with a small sundial on Drew's desk. Finally, Irfin looked up and said almost defensively, "I gave her a protection device and she left. However, I am concerned for her safety."

"Why didn't you stop her?" Drew demanded.

"She is an adult faerie and in case you didn't notice, quite strong in her opinions. Anyway, leprechauns are not welcome where she went."

"Where did she go?"

"Isidghe."

"Where is that?"

Irfin scratched his head. "Isidghe is generally a temporary dwelling in mossy cracks in rocks and tree roots." His piercing eyes met Drew's. "It's a realm just above the dark creatures. She went to the land of the goblins."

"Goblins. You're serious?" Fear for Pandimora raced through Drew. "Why goblins?"

"Despite their trouble-making reputation, goblins have useful skills. Long ago they learned how to shift matter. They are the only species of the fae who don't use portals. She hopes they will help her gain undetected access to Aisywel."

"Shift matter. Is that like teleporting? Like something out of Star Trek?"

Irfin nodded. "In a way, but without the modern technology."

∞ Chapter Seven ∞

Pandimora stood in the sharp-edged red grass. The damp soil between her bare toes stained her feet a dull, washed-out blue and she could feel it seeping under her toenails. She found Isidghe wonderfully unique and vibrantly alive, the blue soil abounding with low-growing, lushly flowering plants.

The brilliance of the two and a half suns in the sky was not something she'd expected, and instead of a shadowy place, she found the translucent green sky a pleasant surprise.

Isidghe: the land of upside down, home to goblins of every nature, size and disposition. She hoped she'd arrived on a very good day, because everyone knew goblins had manners and worse habits even on their best days. On a bad day, they could be quite obnoxious if they took a dislike to you. The up-side to coming here was that goblins had an abundance of energy to shift matter at whim. The question remained, would they allow her to harness their energy to propel herself into Aisywel to find her sister?

"Why are you sneaking about?" The disgruntled voice came from behind her.

Calmly, Pandimora turned. "I've just arrived," she said, searching for the source of the voice.

"And already trespassing," the voice snapped.

Suddenly a tree sprouted beside Pandimora, growing eye level with her, and on the top spindly branch sat a small orange goblin with an immense, protruding stomach. His ears were large and his eyes very small. The goblin regarded her with a mixture of interest and suspicion. Several spike-like protrusions stuck out from its hairless skull.

"I meant no trespass or intrusion. I was listening to the air around me to find my way."

"Listening to the air?" the goblin said incredulously.

Pandimora tilted her head and admitted quietly, "Yes."

The goblin put back its head and began to laugh. It had tiny stubs of brownish gums, so at least Pandimora need not worry about being bitten. When the goblin at last stopped laughing, she noted its small protruding eyes were of the most lovely shade of purple. He laced his long thin fingers over his rounded stomach and rocked back and forth on the tree limb. "And why would a faerie come all the way from Aisywel?"

Surprised, Pandimora said, "How did you know?"

"That you're from Aisywel? A sugary sweetness

swirls in the air around you. It's rare to have an Aisywel faerie take an interest in our dear little world," he ended sarcastically.

"Your world is full of colorful delights and quite beautiful. I have to admit I'm puzzled why the goblins roam the earth realm in the dark of night when it's so much more pleasant here." She waved her arm toward the scarlet flowering bushes that began to pop up out of the ground around them. She reached down and gently touched a blood-red petal. "It is quite different than I expected."

"Yeah, we get that a lot," he drawled, sounding bored. "Why are you here?" he said, dispensing with the chit-chat.

"I need to get into Aisywel. The search for the truth led me here to seek your skills in shifting matter."

A devilish gleam entered his eyes and his smile turned sly. "The truth? That can be quite a slippery slope. What if I told you when you arrived here, you breathed our goblin mist and the truth is you are dreaming this conversation while fast asleep over there?" He pointed to a spot beyond where they stood. "See, look over there. Fast asleep in that brackish swamp."

Pandimora looked, her heart rate picking up just a bit. She saw shallow gray water, small bugs crawling along its surface, and what looked like a woman wearing clothes similar to her own short top and pants lying on her side, her face pillowed against her bent arm. Abundant red hair floated along the water's surface.

Her stomach muscles tensed, but she shook her

head. "I don't believe that's me." She put her arms behind her back and pinched her wrist, hard.

"But how do you know? You could be dreaming this entire conversation right now."

"If that is true, I shall review it for helpful tidbits when I awaken," she said, shrugging with pretended unconcern then pinched her wrist again for good measure.

"Hmm." He cupped his small orange chin with a finger and thumb. "You're not a typical Aisywel faerie, now are you? I was sure you would scuttle over there as quick as could be and shake yourself awake."

Pandimora nodded. "You're right, I'm not a typical faerie." She hoped he could not tell that her knees were shaking. If she had not pinched herself to make sure she wasn't dreaming, she would indeed have been tempted to go shake herself awake.

He jumped up and down on the skinny branch, which bowed under his weight. "All right then," he snapped. "So you've come to this lowly place for answers unfound? Tell me your questions, and keep in mind they may be important to you, but not to me. If you bore me I will pop you right out of here."

His cross purple eyes warned her not to rile him. "I understand," she said quickly. "Let me introduce myself. I am Pandimora. I need to get back into Aisywel so I can find my sister. I also seek the truth about my family who disappeared when I was young." She did not think it prudent to tell him she was also in search of the lost crystal.

The goblin opened his eyes very wide and

gripped the skinny tree trunk as his feet slipped down the branch on which he stood. "That's a lofty goal for a faerie, known to merely frolic under the light of the moon without care or worry. Have you been banned from Aisywel, then?" He regained his balance, smiled with delight and put his fingers together, twiddling the fingertips together quickly.

Reluctantly, she nodded.

"I see, I see. And so you have come here. Little faerie, why do you think the goblins will help you? I have no aversion to faeries, but really, we don't share the same sense of fairness or values. Just imagine if I were to show up in Aisywel looking for you." He pretended to shudder and rolled his eyes. "Imagine the reaction."

"My soul gift is finding that which is lost. I dreamt of the goblins in my search for the truth."

"How very enterprising of you." He appeared to frown. "Look at it this way. Perhaps your family knows where they are and you're the only one who is really missing."

"This is very serious, Goblin."

He heaved a deep sigh. "And what will you do once you gain access? You could go up in a puff of smoke. Give a good answer or I will be gone in a flash and you will be left asleep in that marsh."

Pandimora swallowed, a little intimidated at the thinly veiled threat, but she had to persevere. "I am the daughter of Declan, high lord of the faeries, and Clare, white witch of the earth realm."

He narrowed his eyes. "Child of a faerie and a human witch." He put his hands on his hips. "That is quite a story."

"It is the truth," she said quietly.

Just then there was a rustling through the long, sharp grasses and another goblin appeared, this one blue with small, irregularly shaped pink markings along its entire naked body.

"Sirt has arrived," said the first goblin, grinning gleefully. He tossed her a sidelong glance. "He's not fond of faeries, you know."

Much taller than the orange goblin, Sirt was thin with long spindly arms and legs and very large feet. As he approached there was a suctioning sound and Pandimora realized he had suction-cup-like feet that gripped the moist ground.

"Who have you captured, Jonic?" Sirt inquired with what Pandimora thought was only mild interest.

"An Aisywel faerie," replied the orange goblin Jonic. "Surely you can smell the sugar sweetness all around us? Can you imagine her showing up here asking questions?"

"What kind of questions?"

Pandimora quickly stepped back as the goblin Sirt moved to face her, his long arms swinging out from his body as he straightened from a slouched position. "And who are you to demand anything?" He looked at Jonic, then back at her. He waved his hands. "No, no, you must go away. We cannot have faeries arriving willy-nilly asking questions --" But suddenly he stopped, his mouth hanging open as his glance fell to her arm. Pandimora looked down at her arm also.

"The elven star," Sirt said, his voice changing. He looked accusingly at Jonic. "You didn't say she had the star."

"You were hiding it!" Jonic said accusingly. "Show it to us," he ordered, his eyes lit with excitement. He poked her arm with a thin finger. "It was once a mark of protection," he added. He tilted his head. "How very odd it looks."

Pandimora tamped down her excitement. "How do you know that?"

"You escaped Aisywel, did you not? The elder doesn't have you in his sight." He traced the points of the star with a fingertip. "Here is the original eight-pointed star."

To her amazement the original elven star appeared on her arm.

"And here is the current marking." And as he retraced the points, it became twelve points again instead of eight.

"Yes." She nodded. "What else can you tell me?"

With a mercurial change of mood, Sirt's mouth changed to a straight, uncompromising line. "We don't have the answers you want. Leave now before we lock you up somewhere dark."

"Why can't you tell me?" she asked, but the goblins turned their backs to her.

"Leave!" Sirt's voice swirled around her.

Pandimora looked behind her, seeing the crisp outline of the portal. In frustration, she wondered if they wouldn't help her where else could she go?

"I need help getting into Aisywel," she said, not moving.

The tall goblin turned back to her. "Are you still here?"

"If you were kicked out, you can't go back," Jonic,

the orange goblin, said with certainty.

"But you can shift matter. What will it take for you to help me?"

"Too dangerous," said Sirt.

"Be on your way," said Jonic.

Pandimora turned and walked back through the tall grass, now interspersed with the beautiful flowers, feeling the bite of the grasses against her bare feet.

A soft snicker sounded behind her. "She gave up easily, didn't she, Sirt?" Something wet slapped Pandimora between the shoulder blades.

Surprised, she turned quickly and a wet blob hit her knee. Jonic held a blob of blue mud in one hand.

Keeping both goblins in sight, she bent down and scooped up her own fistful of the blue goo. With a laugh, she flung it, splattering both goblins across the neck and cheeks. The blue blobs of dirt stood out brightly on Jonic's orange skin.

"All I want are answers," she said.

"Answers are like gold," said Jonic. He scooped up another handful. Pandimora ducked and the blue mud flew past her head.

She had to make one more effort. "Will you help me?"

"Not today and maybe not tomorrow," Sirt declared with gleeful mischief.

She eyed the mud in his hands, twisting to the side, but the mud hit her softly so that her pants and blouse were now a sodden blue mess.

"You'd better leave now. We can't be bothered with your silly questions." The goblin's expression turned sober, and they dropped the remainder of their mud.

"We don't do business with faeries," Sirt hissed.

"Maybe we'll help you tomorrow," said Jonic. Pandimora looked from Sirt to Jonic.

"There are no guarantees when a goblin tells you anything." Jonic added, his hands on his rounded hips.

Sirt nodded his head. "That's right, no guarantees. Be off, faerie."

She knew half-truths were a goblin's way of life. "I will wait and maybe you'll change your mind."

"No," they both said in unison.

"Come back later, at midnight," said Jonic. "Unless you're afraid of the dark. It gets very dark here. There are no delightful fireflies to light your path," and both goblins laughed, hopping along behind as she walked toward the portal.

"I won't be afraid," she said, wondering if that were entirely true. "And after dark, won't the goblins be in the earth realm?"

They did not deign to reply, but she noticed they were staring again at the star on her arm.

She held out her arm. "Can you tell me more about this elven star?"

Silence.

Pandimora persevered. "Do you know my brother Kirklas?"

Sirt looked at the other goblin and rolled his eyes. "There's no resonance or reverberations from his energy even in our world. There are higher realms than Isidghe, of course, but his aura has not been in energy since the night of the disappearance. It was said the high lord of the faeries was preparing him to take his place all those years ago."

Tension squeezed between Pandimora's shoulders. "But he must be alive," she murmured, feeling her own desperation.

"Why must he be?" retorted Jonic. Sirt remained silent, his expression doubtful.

Pandimora clenched her hands.

The goblins skittered in even closer and Sirt crooked his finger for her to bend down. "Kirklas is the rightful heir," he whispered. "You gather information as you will, but it is Kirklas who bears the responsibility and the marks of everlasting power."

"What mark does my brother bear?"

"Ancient symbols as you and your sister, but also marks of unity and the all-knowing spirals of life. His power can be harnessed only through actions motivated by justice."

Jonic frowned. "Justice! Bah! Revenge is the most fun you can have."

Sirt hit Jonic on the arm and Jonic scrambled to grab a branch to keep from toppling to the ground. "That's what gets you into trouble and that's why goblins are forced to roam the earth at night -- thinking like that!"

Revenge, Pandimora thought. That word made her feel very cold. Revenge for what was done to their family. "If he seeks revenge ..." she let her voice trail off as a shiver swept through her.

"He will be lost forever. Not only to his family, but to himself."

"And my parents?" she finally asked with barely a sliver of hope.

"You can always try Dinorma," Sirt said. "Don't plan on staying there too long, though. Faeries are not well tolerated."

Dinorma, the wasteland of the lost. She knew the faeries of Aisywel had no connection with the lost of Dinorma. It was the most dangerous place a faerie could go. Even she was not brave enough to go to that dimension.

Suddenly she noticed the portal's odd glow. Someone was attempting to breach the portal.

"Goodbye," she said quickly. Would Irfin attempt to enter the goblin world? As a sorcerer he would not be tolerated here; the goblins hated sorcerers because of an ancient feud. She couldn't allow him to be placed in harm's way. Pandimora ran toward the portal but it moved further away from her and she heard the goblins mischievous laughter following her.

***

"I didn't tell you where Pandimora was so that you could endanger your life," Irfin said irritably.

Drew stared at the portal outline. "I don't plan to endanger her life. Tell me what to do."

Irfin heaved a sigh. "I can see there's no changing your mind. Run into the portal, but don't hesitate or it'll bounce you right back out."

"That's not how Pandimora does it." Drew stared at the eight-foot high portal Irfin had materialized in his office hallway. Luckily he had nine-foot ceilings.

Irfin waved his hand impatiently. "That's because she's faerie and of a lighter vibration. Humans have no choice but to rush forward." He hesitated then cleared his throat. "Mmm, now --

there's one more thing. If you see a goblin, don't say a word. In fact, if you can stay out of sight. They're not fond of humans."

"I'm sure the feeling is mutual," Drew said. He wondered when he'd stopped being amazed that faeries existed and that they used portals like humans hopped trains. And now Pandimora was somewhere beyond that portal in a place where goblins lived. What if they didn't let her leave?

Drew watched the fluctuating outline of the portal, brown with a tinge of green along the edges. It wobbled like gelatin. With a last look at Irfin he jumped feet first into the center and landed on the other side, falling to his knees in gooey blue stuff. Looking around, he was immediately disoriented as everything looked disconcertingly upside down.

He stared in awe at a translucent green sky with what appeared to be two suns, aware of distant rumblings like thunder. Drew lunged almost drunkenly to his feet, weirdly off balance. Pandimora ran toward him and he could see her panicked expression. Drew stood, prepared to run to meet her when he realized there were a dozen or more ugly, frightening creatures of all sizes and appearances giving chase behind her.

Goblins. Heart hammering, Drew lurched toward her, reaching out to grab her hand. "Hurry!" he yelled. "You're being chased." The mob behind her could have been a scene from a horror movie.

He turned back to the portal, but somehow it was further away than he'd imagined and it kept bouncing backwards. He ran as hard as he could, Pandimora's hand in his, and then suddenly she passed him and hauled him along behind her. He had all he could do to keep up with her petite frame as her slim legs moved like pistons.

The goblins were almost on them. He moved even faster, pushing himself to the limit. They were not going to get her. His free hand pressed against the medallion in his pocket. Irfin's device. Knowing it was worth a shot, he squeezed the device. Nothing happened. "Really?"

He looked back. A long spindly goblin arm reached out to Pandimora. Drew slowed down to intercept the creature, but Pandimora pulled him hard toward her. God! she was strong. His feet left the ground and then he landed and ran again. Frantically, he pressed the device again.

Pandimora gave a hard tug and propelled both of them into the portal and they tumbled through and out the other side. Drew landed on the wood floor of his office and rolled, arms around Pandimora, cradling her protectively. Their momentum brought them against the wall and Drew grunted at the impact of the hard wood against his back. At the rate he was slamming into walls, he'd have to make an appointment for a chiropractic adjustment.

Pandimora immediately shoved him away and jumped to her feet.

"Hey --" he said as he slid across the floor. She was strong!

Standing over him, hands on her hips, she looked beautiful ... and furious, her clear blue eyes shooting angry sparks toward him. Drew blinked. Holy cow.

"What have you done?" she demanded.

"I got you out of harm's way," he said, annoyed.

"You may have ruined everything I accomplished," she snapped.

Drew came to his feet. "You were in danger."

"I was not!"

"Irfin said --"

She looked around. "Where is he? I will have a word with him."

"Why are you so angry? I got us out of there in time -- did something terrible happen with those goblins?"

"It could have. You have no idea the danger. You don't enter a world you know nothing about. The goblins could have taken you to a dark hole and I can't even envision the torment they'd heap upon a human for daring to enter their realm."

"Wait a second. You're angry because I could have been hurt?"

She glared at him.

"This isn't about me," Drew said. "I saw them, they were after you. If it wasn't for this device --" He pulled Irfin's device from his pocket and waved it.

"No!" she retorted, not even glancing at the medallion, impatiently shoving her red braid over her shoulder. "I was leaving quietly. The goblins were fine until you showed up. They were after you. You!"

"What?" They hadn't been chasing her?

She paced away from him. "Now I'm not sure they'll allow my return."

"Why would you want to go back?"

"They might have helped me shift into Aisywel."

"Irfin told me --" he tried a different tack. "I thought you were in danger. And after seeing those goblins --" It had been an eerie experience, seeing real life goblins chasing her -- or him.

"They became incensed when they smelled a human," she said, obviously trying to hold back her temper. "I was trying to bargain with them."

Drew's uneasiness increased. "What kind of bargain? Not like with your soul or something?"

Pandimora looked at him incredulously then shook her head. "You watch too much television."

A short laugh escaped him. "And what do you know about television?"

She placed her hands on her hips and glowered at him. "Drew, you cannot distract me from my anger."

"I can feel it," he said ruefully. "It's practically burning the clothes off my back." He sighed. "Listen, this is all new to me. Irfin had me convinced you were in trouble. So I took a leap of faith and jumped the portal."

She folded her arms. "Again."

"Yeah, you're right. Again." He cleared his throat. Had Irfin set him up? His earlier suspicion rose again. Was Irfin hiding something that could endanger both of them? "Pandimora, can we talk about this? I want to help." He held up a hand. "But only where you want me to. I really thought you were in mortal danger."

A little more patiently, she said, "In my world, humans are fragile. But what I fear is you will not hesitate to interfere again if you misunderstand a situation."

Drew had a feeling she was right.

"All right, I get that you're self-sufficient and

intelligent and know everything about these worlds and I know nothing -- and you don't need me interfering." That was a lot to admit for a guy used to taking charge.

She looked at him in surprise. "Drew, I do not know everything about these worlds, but whether you like it or not, being human puts you at a disadvantage."

"I get it," he said, clenching his jaw. "Can you at least tell me what happened? It wasn't my intention to screw up your mission. I was damned worried."

"Irfin --" she looked around his office, still searching for the little man.

"He appears to be gone," Drew said grimly. "This is a small office and there's no place to hide. Aren't you cold? You're soaking wet," he said, indicating the blue splotches all over her clothes and hair, blue stains running down her neck. His protective instincts rose again, even though she'd proven she could take care of herself.

Pandimora sighed and some of the angry stiffness seemed to leave her. "There was mud thrown." She gripped his arm, her strength surprising him considering she was such a petite woman -- faerie, he reminded himself. "First, I will get your promise you will not jump again into a world you know nothing about. You could be killed or worse. And I don't care what Irfin said, I was fine."

He decided he didn't need to know what could be worse than being dead in another dimension. "I'll do my best not to interfere," he promised reluctantly. Maybe he'd be able to keep the promise.

Pandimora moved away, then restlessly sat down in his desk chair. "There were two goblins, Sirt and Jonic. They threw mud at me. But it was merely a way to indicate their acceptance of me in their world, for a short time. There was no threat."

"And yet they have no problem coming here and trying to scare people to death."

She brushed that aside. "They come here because they can and it is based on an ancient agreement."

Drew could see they were on two different wavelengths. "Have you been to Isidghe before?" he asked.

"No."

"What I saw would give anyone nightmares."

She put her arms around herself. "You must never return there, Drew, especially since they have your scent."

"I'm worried for your safety. And after seeing what the elder is capable of --"

Alarmed, she reached for his hand. "The elder came after you? You must not admit to any knowledge of me or he'll take you away."

"Irfin arrived and he took off," he said quickly. "Will the goblins help you?"

She chewed her lip. "Perhaps, if I go back at the midnight hour."

He looked at his watch. Almost nine-forty.

"I was trying to get them to agree to help me shift matter so I could sneak back into Aisywel. I can't lose hope, but no one has been aware of my brother's vibration since the time he disappeared. I've never experienced such turmoil within my heart."

Drew, used to taking charge of situations, hesitated. Thinking he might have screwed up her plans didn't sit well with him. He watched her get up, saw the frustration in her beautiful eyes, then she turned and walked back toward the door. He wanted to do whatever he could to protect her, but in reality he couldn't stop her if she chose to keep walking. She paused by the outer door to the street and then began to go through the door.

"Wait," he said, following her. "It's late. At least put on dry clothes. My partner Sara has an office in the back and will have something you can wear. I don't think she'd mind." Tensely, he waited for her response.

Pandimora turned and met his gaze. "I suspect I know why Irfin sent you after me," she said abruptly.

"You do?" He had his own suspicions regarding Irfin. He was getting the feeling Irfin wanted him out of the way.

She nodded grimly. "He wants me distracted from returning to Aisywel, so he's matchmaking."

Again, she'd totally surprised him. Drew lifted a brow. "That's the last thing I expected you to say. And how do you feel about that?" How did he feel about being matched with Pandimora? Warmth released some of the tension in his stomach, but then he withdrew that thought. They were from two different worlds.

Her full lips curved in a slight smile. "We played together as children and now I see you as a man, Drew. I have thought about you for a long time, but

..." she shrugged, "there is so much separating us. You here in your dimension, and if I ever get back to Aisywel ..."

He supposed she was right, but that didn't stop him from wanting to close the space between them and pull her into his arms. Just the thought made a light sweat break out on his forehead. He had the idea making love with Pandimora would be an out-of-this-world experience.

Instead, he said, "Do you think he wants to prevent you from finding the truth about your family? What do you really know about him?"

Pandimora looked surprised. "Irfin is of the fae," she said simply, as if that were explanation enough.

"So is the elder," Drew said dryly. "Listen, I don't want to argue. How about dry clothes and we can go to my place until you have to leave? We can get something to eat," Drew added. He wanted to grab as much time as he could with her. "You do eat, right?"

She smiled for the first time that night. "Of course."

Persuasively, he added, "It's not like you have to be here to access a portal, right? You can do it from my apartment?"

She nodded in agreement. "There is nowhere in any dimension I cannot access a portal."

Drew didn't have the heart to remind her that was true -- except for her home, Aisywel.

∞ Chapter Eight ∞

Irfin remained suspended between worlds, seeing the threat against Pandimora had lessened for the moment, but in truth his first concern was locating the lost crystal. He frowned, wondering how the faerie realm had become so twisted and dangerous. In ancient times all one had to worry about were the battles and skirmishes fought in the open and with weapons he could easily disarm.

Now, Pandimora was exiled from her home and her family missing, possibly forever. He frowned. Kirklas was lost and perhaps still immortal, his soul burning bright with anger and a thirst for revenge, but as to where he might be ...

Irfin's mission to restore the lost crystal burned deeply. He could not predict the outcome for Pandimora. He knew the power Lukais held and he had no wish to go against the elder.

Pandimora could triumph and survive or just as

easily be crushed and he knew if she and her siblings were crushed, the faerie realms would soon also cease to exist. The strength of their souls, Kirklas being the last in line as the lord of the faeries, could well determine the outcome for all faerie realms.

This night, Irfin turned to his earth family, watching them, his dear Mary with barely enough life force pulsing to keep her alive. He allowed time's memory to slip into the past when he first knew her. Only in the rich dreaming state could he go back to that time and interact with her as she used to be.

Regret caught Irfin by surprise. If only he had lived his long, eventful life more wisely. He thought of Drew's words that his wife merely wanted him home, not hunting for a cure. Irfin closed his eyes. He'd gone too far in this quest, there was no turning back. When they found the lost crystal, everything would change.

***

Drew rubbed his forehead, staring at the computer screen. He glanced at the time. Ten-forty. He'd immersed himself in faerie tales and folklore, surfing the internet for information, anything that might give him a clue about the world Pandimora inhabited. He'd found a plethora of information, probably ninety-eight percent of it fiction and he'd come to the conclusion sifting through it all for facts would be a nearly impossible task. And when he'd come to the goblin information, his blood chilled. The descriptions were all similar; mischievous, evil and malevolent. They were considered the darker side of the faerie kingdom and from the little he'd seen he could well believe it.

He pulled out the file on Rick Martin, aka Irfin, staring at the photos of the man. Leprechaun and sorcerer in the faerie realm, human persona on earth. It just all felt too crazy and impossible to be real.

And now Irfin might be helping the elder Lukais toward world domination or whatever it was the elder had planned. If he had as much power as Pandimora claimed, and wanted more, it was feasible he'd try to hide his actions to keep everyone fooled.

Drew rubbed his eyes as they burned. Pandimora would be leaving soon and maybe this time he wouldn't see her again. She didn't seem to need help to find her family. And yet he'd sensed her vulnerability even if only for a minute or so earlier when she'd talked about the wrong done to her loved ones. Drew couldn't imagine his own family being ripped apart as hers had been.

He'd left voice messages for his parents. His brother Grey was on vacation this week, and his phone had remained busy: no doubt the lines were down due to the increasing ferocity of the weather. Sara's cell went straight to voicemail. It was like she'd dropped off the face of the earth. She had proven well able to take care of herself, but he worried about her. He hoped she was holed up somewhere on a case and hadn't been caught in any of this mess.

How would he explain the missing week? That he'd spent it with a faerie who had lost her family and slipped in and out of dimensions that humans can't see or access?

Drew glanced at his phone as it began to vibrate. An out of state number, perhaps the crystal expert whose name had cropped up in his research and whom he'd called earlier.

"Drew here."

"Julie Matters returning your call. I hope it's not too late. Your message sounded kind of urgent."

"I'm glad you called. I'm a private investigator doing some research on crystals and their history in relation to a case."

"Well, I'll try to help you. What is it you need to know?"

"Have you ever experienced crystals having some kind of power?"

"In holistic medicine crystals and stones are used for healing. Some practitioners swear by this type of healing, while others say it's more of a placebo type effect. The simple answer is that gemstones and crystals have different frequencies that correspond to and can possibly heal different parts of the body."

"Okay, then what about them having powers outside of healing?"

"Can you be more specific?"

He took a deep breath. "Crystals that have the ability to upset weather patterns or they can be harnessed to control magnetic fields, such as some kind of super energy source connecting to power grids." He cleared his throat. "I know this sounds kind of out there."

She hesitated then said, "You're delving into theories by those who believe in Atlantis and the supposedly enormous crystal power they harnessed and aligned on a grid with pyramids. In fact the theory is they grew their own crystals and the very same crystals lie beneath the ground, waiting to be once more activated in various places around the globe. That, by the way, was put forth by Edgar Cayce, a psychic who gave predictions while in a trancelike sleep."

"I came across Cayce in my research. Have you ever heard of holograms being created with a crystal?"

"No, but the idea is intriguing."

"Do you think it's possible?"

"I'm not taking an easy way out here, but I do believe there's a lot we don't know."

"What about crystals so powerful they have the potential to do great damage worldwide?"

"Based on the theory of Atlantis, it's believed power could be wielded with ancient crystals. If you look at Plato's writing, there is plenty of mention of large and powerful crystals which were supposedly in use, again at the time of Atlantis, and we're talking tens of thousands of years ago." She paused. "Do I believe it's possible to harness incredible power with a large enough crystal? Yes. But then I happen to agree with Plato that Atlantis really did exist. It sounds like you're involved in a really intriguing case," she added.

"That's one way of looking at it," Drew said ruefully. "Quite frankly this case is outside my realm of experience."

"If it helps at all, I can attest to the effectiveness of crystal healing, since I've experienced it myself.

I've studied crystals and their properties for many years and I really can't discount there is a certain power they wield. However, if the legends about Atlantis are true, the crystals were misused and that's one of the reasons the continent of Atlantis was destroyed. It's thought it was swept away through a tsunami or some cataclysmic event."

"One last question. Do you know of any research linking faeries and crystals?"

"I have personally seen faeries but I don't know anything about them utilizing crystals."

"You've seen them?" Drew asked, surprised.

"A long time ago certainly. I grew up in Iceland. There we call them the hidden people and it's rather taken for granted they live there among us. Even our roads and new construction make way for known homes or mounds of the hidden people. It's not to say everyone fully believes in them, but the majority don't discount them either."

"Thanks again for your input," he said.

"I hope I've helped in some regard. Call again if other questions arise. And one more thing Drew."

"Yes?"

"Since this has been an extraordinary conversation anyway, I want to leave you with a word of caution: unless you're prepared for havoc in your life, don't anger the faeries."

"Thanks." Too late, he thought.

***

Drew paused in the bedroom doorway, staring at the window as ice pellets hit the glass. Pandimora slept in his bed, snuggled down into the bedcovers and pillows. His first instinct was to gather her into his arms, make love to her all night, but his brain remained at odds with his heart. Irfin had been the first to tell him it wasn't easy merging two such divergent lifestyles. Drew ran a hand over the back of his neck. It was too soon anyway to even think about anything like that, but his mind just kept wandering there.

And what if she had inherited her mother's mental illness? Did he even want to deal with such a situation again after the fiasco of his marriage to Deborah?

Supposedly her mother was human, but he had no timeline as to when she'd lived here, or even a last name. As far as he could figure out Pandimora's age was the equivalent of about one hundred and seventy years his time. Did that mean her mother lived that long ago when she'd decided to leave earth to be with Declan in Aisywel?

Drew admired Pandimora's willingness to find the truth but he was really worried for her, and he wasn't looking forward to another confrontation with the elder. Too bad he didn't have a crystal to fight with and even the odds. From the little he'd interacted with the elder, he knew he'd have to fight smarter with someone so powerful; he just hadn't figured that part out yet.

Drew looked at his watch. Eleven twenty-four. He toyed with the idea of allowing her to sleep through the midnight hour and therefore miss returning to the land of the goblins. It didn't sit right with him that she would return to such a dangerous place. He put his head back, knowing he couldn't mess up her plan to find her family. He'd help her however he could, even in his limited human way.

And where the heck was Irfin? He still had to wonder if he'd set him up by sending him into goblin territory. Maybe the little man was playing with both of them.

He moved to the bed and settled down beside her, pulling the blanket over both of them. He turned on his side and stared at her, wondering how this would all turn out. Drew closed his eyes for a moment, seeing again those angry, distorted creatures chasing behind Pandimora. Talk about nightmares. That was his last thought before he, too, drifted off to sleep.

***

Gracefully, Pandimora rose from the bed, sitting up to stare at her reflection in a mirror. Frowning, she leaned closer, seeing a wavering image taking shape under the shining mirror's surface. She put her fingers against the mirror and into the glass as the face became clearer. It was her own face, but with the wrinkles of age. She frowned, surprised to see her face in such a way as she had never imagined it.

"It's me," she whispered. The face rippled in the glass like a pebble cast into water.

Emotions of fear and abandonment rushed through Pandimora as she thought of the loss of her family. Her parents, brother, and possibly her sister. She put a hand to her mouth, catching her breath.

The mirror began to crack in small sections, and then it shattered, shiny glass covering her hands and wrists. She saw fires burning deep beneath the earth's surface. The core's heat encircled her as she entered a deep cavern, dark with curved stone ceilings, faces of the past painted high on the dark walls. Beautiful, sparkling crystals hung from the cavern ceiling. As she attempted to focus on her new surroundings, everything shifted and slid away. Pandimora shook the glass from her hands, stared at a spot of scarlet welling on the back of her hand. Blood of the fae.

"Find the crystal lost to time." Irfin's voice wove around her. "You will have the answers you seek."

Pandimora pinched her wrist and jerked as lightning crackled around her. Disoriented, she stared around the semi-darkened room, her gaze coming to rest on Drew, who lay beside her in the bed. A dream. She was in his bedroom and awake. It had been a dream.

"Beneath the earth's surface," she murmured. Pandimora leaned toward Drew, his scent in her nostrils. This man, this human, had been in her heart through all the time she had known him. So many years she had watched his life and his struggles, and he had not known. She had tried to stay away.

He'd loved a human, but something had fractured that relationship. And then Pandimora had come to sneak a peek into his life and found him once more alone.

Drew was a man unlike any she had known in the faerie realm. To her, his essence felt so raw and physical, a light contained within a human frame. His sense of duty urged him to help her, but she knew it would be too dangerous. She wondered about her own aged face she'd seen in the dream. Was it an indication of a possible future? But how could that be? Faeries did not age as represented in the dream.

Pandimora gazed across the room at the ice hitting the glass windows. The energy of the discord in the faerie realm affected the earth weather. She knew it would only get worse as time went on. Unless ...unless something occurred to calm the energy being unleashed. Was Lukais responsible for this abundance of chaotic energy or could it be her own tortured quest that charged the air as long as she remained here on earth?

Pandimora saw the cavern from her dream. Irfin had urged her to find the crystal lost to time. Going too close to the earth's core would be dangerous, even for a faerie but if she could find the answers she needed about her family it would certainly be worth the risk.

Pandimora twined her fingers gently in Drew's silky dark blond hair. Each time she left Drew the possibility existed she might not return. Might never see Drew again. The thought made her heart heavy.

She touched her fingers gently to his jaw, saw the blue sparks where their skin touched.

His eyes snapped open and he was alert and instantly awake. His eyes searched hers, feeling like a physical touch, then he glanced at the bedside clock. "I fell asleep. It's almost midnight," he said, stifling a yawn.

She shook her head. "Drew, going back to the goblins now is no longer a concern. We faeries dream richly, and I have seen in my dreams where I need to go."

"Aisywel?"

"In time, yes." Lightly, she traced the groove of his lean cheek. "I must leave soon, but it would make me sad if I didn't do this now," she whispered, leaning down to touch his lower lip with the tip of her tongue. "I hope you don't mind if I kiss you." She closed her eyes, enjoying the sensation of touching him. "I wish to make love with you, but sadness fills me because it will never be more than this moment."

Drew brushed his nose against hers. "And I'd love to make love to you, too, Pandimora," he said. He lightly gripped her hands. "What are you planning?"

She kissed him to forestall more questions. "Intimate encounters are discouraged with those outside the world of the fae, but I cannot let this opportunity slip away." She needed to gauge his reaction. If he didn't wish to be with her, she would gracefully withdraw now.

He sat upright, leaned back against the headboard, opening his arm so she could move into the shelter of that arm. His pulled her up against him. "That feels good," he said. "All I can think about is you, Pandimora. Even when I'm dreaming, I see you."

"I feel the same," she said. "Knowing I must leave would hurt less, I think, if we didn't feel this attraction."

His gaze sharpened. "Tell me what you're planning."

She drew a deep breath, exhaled. "In my dream, I saw caverns. I can't explain the images, but I know I must go beneath the earth's surface, close to the earth's core." She felt his resistance, knew he didn't want her to expose herself to the danger. Before he could voice the resistance, she said softly, urgently, "Drew, wouldn't you do the same for your family -- do whatever you could to learn the truth -- at any risk to yourself?"

"Yes, but I don't want anything to happen to you. I worry you'll disappear into some dimension and be lost forever. It's not like I can just come and find you." He sighed. "But I also understand about family."

"It has been a difficult time for you, Drew, learning of dimensions you never knew existed. Being attacked by the elder."

He nodded, but he also grinned. "Yeah, but the up-side is, I get to hold a luscious faerie in my arms."

"I am enjoying being held in your arms." Even if it's only once. She pressed her cheek against his chest.

"You should be some guy's love," he said gruffly. "Cherished and protected. But lately it seems you're doing the protecting, yanking me from the clutches of goblins."

She enjoyed the contact with his warm skin. Pandimora had never felt cherished in her life, but now she began to understand what it meant to experience such an emotion.

"I love being here with you Drew. It's almost like we're insulated from the storm outside here inside this room. I feel safe and protected." Her mouth turned down. "I know it's an illusion but for right now I'd like to cherish these moments, let the illusion play itself out. Sometimes, faeries can be too plodding in their approach to life. I'd like to set aside who we are in our own respective worlds and just now be a man and a woman who are attracted to each other." She ran a hand lightly up his shoulder. Drew leaned down to her and kissed her mouth, the slight scratch of his chin against her cheek.

"I need a shave," he said ruefully, rubbing the stubble on his chin.

Pandimora smiled, not minding at all. "It creates abrasion," she said. "Watch the play of light between us." As she rubbed his whiskered cheeks Pandimora read the wonder in his eyes at the blue glow that began to build around them.

"Our interactions have been muted up to now," she said, gently playing her fingers through the blue light. "I have to warn you this energy flow could become very intense." Even now the light moved along the walls.

"I'll handle it," he said, moving to lie flat on his back. He held his hand out for her to join him. Gracefully, she sank into him, twining her arms around his neck. "Drew, that first night when we exchanged energy was a mere shadow of what can happen between a human and faerie."

"If it's anything like when you pulled me away from the goblins -- I know you're very strong." He lifted slightly away and worked his shirt over his head, exposing his bare chest. Fascinated, Pandimora placed both palms flat against his chest, her fingers splaying through the light sprinkling of silky hair.

"You are very strong in your world," she said admiringly, lifting her gaze to meet his. "Faeries are strong but quite different." She frowned. "Perhaps I have always been attracted to you because I'm part human." She shrugged. "I don't know. We do share common ancestry."

"Irfin mentioned something about that." He touched the back of his hand to the soft skin of her cheek. "Your eyes are like this incredible well," he added. "I feel as if I could get lost in them." He half closed his eyes, inhaled. "Irfin said --" he gave a half laugh. "Never mind. I love your scent. All I can think about, looking past your gorgeous blue irises, is that I'm seeing something inside you no man has ever seen before."

"That's the magic of the fae. Do you wish to know how your scent comes to me? It is earthy, like the early sun-warmed soil of Aisywel." Her nostrils flared. "Your scent reminds me of the things I love about my home. A place that kept me grounded for many years, but a place as delightful and full of mystery today as when I was a small child. It always enfolded me gently in its arms. Even when I practiced rebellion and knew I was different from other faeries, it was still the home in my heart. You, Drew, invoke that same type of feeling inside me. So many years I wondered how you lived, how your life here progressed, and from time to time I would come to the earth realm to peek in on your life after you no longer saw us."

"My life was good for many years, Pandimora, but there were equally dark years."

"I know. Even though I only visited from time to time, the knowledge of your life was available to me."

"The dark years were in my short marriage to

Deborah," he said, reserve in his voice. "You know?"

She shook her head gently. "No, that would be an intrusion upon you. But at times I was aware of your earthly pain."

Drew took a deep breath. "Deborah -- my wife, wasn't well. She threatened many times in our four years together to take her life. We separated many times, but I'd always rush to her when she threatened to take her life. The last time I didn't get there in time."

Pandimora gently touched his arm.

Drew pulled back slightly. "I feel a sense of responsibility for her death," he added bluntly. "I left the police force due to money she had embezzled in her job as an accountant. I tried to get her professional help but she didn't want it."

She shook her head. "No one is responsible for the actions of another."

"Irfin said the same thing. I tell myself that but it doesn't lessen the guilt."

"It sounds like Deborah had extreme sadness."

"That's what her doctor said, but it didn't make it any easier." He looked at her curiously. "Can you see into our future?"

"The future as you understand it does not exist in reality, no matter how much you might wish for it. All time happens as we exist here now. What you think of as the past is playing itself out, as well as what you would call future events. However, life in this realm is very uncertain, and now I feel the same about my beloved Aisywel. I never imagined I would be cast away from the only home I knew. I can only hope my home survives the rebellion I fear is coming." She dropped her pensive thoughts and smiled instead. "But for now, I will kiss you here." She pressed her full red lips to his and the sensation created stirrings of desire within her belly. "And here." She kissed the corner of his mouth.

His fingers slid through her hair, still damp with the blue mud and she laughed. "I am still marked by the blue soil of Isidghe."

"Blue looks good on you," he said, smiling. He pulled back slightly. "I want to be honest. I don't know where this will go, if anywhere. I'm still putting the past to rest. Both of our lives are in upheaval."

"I understand, Drew, but it is my choice now isn't it? If you are willing to let me make love to you?" She hesitated.

His arms squeezed her to him, then he dropped his mouth to hers, tracing the outline of her lips. Pandimora closed her eyes at the delicious rush of sensation throughout her body. Her breath caught. So much emotion ... spirals of desire curled through her body, alerting nerve endings. She just wanted to be close to him, her hands on his body and his on hers. How she had longed for this! This might be the only opportunity for them to be together.

Drew stood, his mouth leaving hers. He straightened and his hands went to his belt. Pandimora dropped her feet to the cushioning rug, stood on tiptoe and then putting her arms around his neck, she lifted her legs and put them around his hips, hooking her heels behind him.

Drew cupped her buttocks, lowering his head to kiss her once more. She put her head back as his mouth traveled down her neck, hardly able to breathe, the sensation was so electrifying.

Gently, Drew flaked dried mud from her cheek and turned to walk across the bedroom, Pandimora still latched onto him.

Drew opened a door and entered a large bathroom; toilet, sink and a grand ivory colored bathtub. She unhooked her heels and slowly lowered herself down his body, her toes curling into a thick soft rug the color of scarlet fireflies.

"Would you like me to run a hot bath?" he said. "We can get rid of the mud."

She smiled with surprised delight. "Like the hot springs?"

"Yes."

Pandimora hugged herself. "I would enjoy that. And will you be in the springs with me?" she asked hopefully.

"If you want me, I'm there."

"Yes." Pandimora removed first the borrowed pants and then the shirt.

"I guess faeries don't wear underwear," Drew muttered. She stood naked, her arms by her side, displaying no false modesty or embarrassment. Eagerly, she stepped toward him. Drew pulled her close to him again, sliding his palms over her skin. "I feel like I've found something precious," he said. "I won't ever want to let you go."

Pandimora didn't want to let Drew go either but they both knew circumstances could pull them apart.

***

Pandimora was everything Drew admired in a

woman. Steadfast, smart, strong and not afraid to state her mind. She had courage. He didn't know any other woman who would brave a goblin world. It didn't sit right with him that the elder had tried to scare her by telling her she suffered the same illness as her mother. He'd seen depression at its worst in Deborah and he was hard pressed to see anything similar in Pandimora. Surely he would recognize the signs? What if after all this they found out she was ill and she had imagined or conjured everything that had occurred? Could he handle that type of situation all over again?

And now she stood here as naked as he'd seen her before, but for a moment he felt uncertain. Faeries and humans were a world apart. Would there be disappointment because of the differences in their worlds? Would it extend to making love? He pondered that thought, staring at the woman before him as she bent down to test the bath water as it gushed into his deep tub. Then he smiled and shook his head. Certainly the worlds were the same on some levels. What could they both do but make tonight one to remember?

Playfully, Pandimora tugged at his hand, pulling him down toward her, then gently nibbling his neck and shoulder with her teeth. Her actions sent an electric jolt from his nipples to his groin. Drew put his arms around her and pulled her up against him, their mouths meeting, white heat melding them together. Sparks of light exploded and he opened his eyes, amazed at the thin blue and silver streaks of light zinging all around them, bouncing off the bathroom's pale ivory walls and reflected in the water.

"Water and electricity don't usually mix," he muttered, unbuckling his belt. "I hope we don't get electrocuted." He thumbed the snap on his pants and pushed the zipper down. Shucking his jeans and underwear, he stepped into the tub as did Pandimora. "That light," he murmured. "Is it really electricity?"

She gave a gurgle of laughter. "We create sparks and energy combustion when we are together."

"And this is normal?"

"What does normal mean in a world inhabited by the magic of the fae? We are two live energy beings." She pressed the full length of her body to his and Drew sucked in his breath, knowing sensory overload wasn't far away as her breasts pressed against him. "We're exploring a world often explored in times past between humans and faeries."

"Have you known any faeries that gave up Aisywel to live in my world?" he asked curiously.

Pandimora nodded. "There have been some who felt it was worth such a life change," she said. "Once you make such a decision, there is no going back."

"What about humans living in the faerie realm?"

Pandimora pressed a hot kiss into the curve of his neck. "There is a ceremony where the human is melded to our world. Once this takes place, there is no going back at all. Not even to visit family."

"Really?" He pulled back slightly to look at her, pushing the flame red hair away from her eyes. "And does the human become immortal?"

"Sadly no, although I have heard tales of

immortality being granted on rare occasions in what you would consider ancient times. It was said a faerie loved a human so much she grew listless and ill to think they would never be together. I'm not sure how it occurred, but eventually the human was allowed to meld to our realm. He became immortal, but that is a rare case. Humans have joined our world through time, but they remained mortal and eventually died."

Drew cupped her face, dropping his mouth to hers, loving the sensory experience of her full lips against his own. He traced her lips with his tongue, exploring their soft contours. The heated vapor of the water rose around them in the small room.

Carefully, he guided both of them down into the large tub. He leaned back against the tub, his back muscles aching a bit from the bruising he'd taken that week, but it didn't matter as he pulled her back into him and the hot water surged against them. Gently, he let his hands roam over her breasts and then down over her stomach. The blue light was a gentle play between his chest and her back. "This feels incredible, as if a ball of energy is between my palms and your skin." He kissed his way along her shoulder, her breasts beckoning him.

Pandimora moved restlessly, her breath escaping in little sighs of delight, teasing him, making him eager to feel her reaction to his touch.

"Easy," he said, "easy." He gently pushed the hair from her forehead, then over her shoulders as it fell across his chest. He loved the feel of her flaming hair against him, the fiery color having a brilliant life of its own.

As big as the tub was, water sloshed precariously close to the edge as Pandimora turned to face him.

"I don't want easy," she murmured and he felt himself going deeper and deeper as he lost himself in her eyes. He needed to remain focused but he just had a feeling he wanted to let go and see where this new experience would take them.

"I have waited a long time for this moment, Drew. I want to be greedy right now, bury myself in your scent and your body inside mine. I feel the temperature rising so beautifully, we fit together so well, and I know this must be the way it is meant to be."

She encircled his erection, took it in her hands and Drew felt himself grow even harder as she touched him tenderly, carefully, then pressed harder and harder. She met his eyes. "I want you inside me now, Drew."

"Pandimora -- protection. Let me get a condom -- "

She pressed a finger to his mouth. "The fae are free of ailments, Drew, and as for becoming with child, that will be my choice in time. So there is no need to worry." Weightlessly, she sank down onto him, the water cushioning, flowing in gentle laps around them. Drew thrust inside her body as she opened her legs to welcome him. She pushed down on him, pulling him in slowly at first then faster. Drew rode the unbelievable sensation of their bodies reacting off each other, the heat of the water and its buoyancy adding to the incredible sensation of weightlessness.

Faster, faster, thrusting, her heated flesh closing

around him. He felt as if he'd come home, as if a certain rightness had brought him to this moment. He'd never encountered such a feeling before, but there was no time to rationalize because the blue lights were fully embracing them, going crazy as she circled her hips in rhythm, jerked toward him and gasped. He kissed her open mouth, their tongues dueling as she pushed harder, sending both of them toward the back of the tub, water sloshing everywhere.

Drew put his hands out to steady them, his chest heaving as his adrenalin raced.

She laughed aloud. "Come to me, Drew. Give me everything."

Their glances locked and Drew tumbled down and down as sensation pulled them together into an abyss of pleasure. One crest after another, an orgasm that shook them, keeping them locked in each other's arms for endless moments, riding the feeling long after the last ripple of sensation slowly dissipated. He could barely catch his breath, his body still pulsed, but he lifted a hand to cup the back of her head, leaning down to gently kiss her lips and then down further, his tongue caressing first one nipple and then the other. Pandimora shuddered with renewed pleasure and moved against him, clamping her legs around his erection as he grew hard once more.

Droplets of water clung to her breasts, beading there, then running in tiny rivulets over the dusky, enticing peaks. Drew swallowed, his gaze caught on the sight of her luscious skin. The tail of her braid was a bright swathe against one breast, the ends curling around her nipple.

***

Pandimora flicked her tongue against Drew's, twined her tongue with his, then she traced his lips.

Drew tightened his butt muscles and arched, lifting both of them upward, once, twice. She wriggled her hips and settled more firmly on him, the sensation an arrow of need spearing through her. Drew cupped her breasts, caressing them and she felt him grow even harder inside her.

She closed her eyes, savoring the multitude of sensations. She bit the corner of her lip, gave a small sigh, and felt even more gloriously alive as Drew kissed her again. White hot sensations clawed at her as an inner explosion of need jumped through every muscle.

She rocked against him, her hands capturing his and holding them on either side of his head at the back of the tub, now holding his larger wrists.

She had a difficult time hanging on to lucid thought and the blue light was starting to go wild all around them with a rhythm all its own, adding vibrancy to their lovemaking. Hazily, she also saw strings of gold light encircling them.

She loved the ride, the buildup, the momentum increasing as did the friction and heat between them.

They kissed hotly, open mouth, tongue to tongue.

"You're so giving," he murmured.

"You make it easy."

She moved torturously slow, then faster and more wildly, her hair flying around them.

Drew's breath sounded ragged. He arched his

hips up, tirelessly setting a smooth, fast rhythm. The blue and gold light became almost blinding so she closed her eyes and just let the sensation bombard every bit of her.

Faster he thrust into her body, and she met him with her own strength, her head back as she said his name. Then everything shattered, the air around them erotically charged. He caught her on either side of her hips, lifted her up, then she plunged down and all thought skittered away as they became a jumbled mass of nerve endings and exploding sensations.

Reality slipped away and pulled her into a timeless space where for an infinitesimal moment, all souls were the same.

∞ Chapter Nine ∞

Drew rubbed his eyes with the heel of his hands. He lay still, feeling strangely disoriented and dizzy. Slowly, recollection began to filter through him. What had happened? They had fallen asleep after the most intense lovemaking he'd ever experienced.

Drew smiled, feeling her warm body curled against him, her breathing steady as she slept. Gently, he touched her breast, brushed his fingers against her arm. Feeling intensely satisfied, he opened his eyes.

He jerked upright, shocked. He grabbed his head, which felt like it was on fire. Something was wrong: very, very wrong. They were no longer in his bedroom or even in his home, but in some kind of cave. Gray, striated rock rose all around them, black horizontal lines scoring the cavern walls. A killer headache as if he'd pulled a drunken all-nighter, something he hadn't done since he was a teenager.

"Pandimora." He shook her gently. "Pandimora. Wake up." Drew's eyes adjusted to the muted light as she began to stir and stretch. "Do you know where we are?" he asked.

Pandimora also bolted upright, then fell back against him, pressing her hand against her forehead. Drew steadied her. "Easy," he said. "I felt disoriented when I first woke up, too." He pressed a palm against the smooth reddish surface under them, feeling the stone's warmth. In fact, the cave itself felt very warm, and maybe that was fortunate considering he wore only a pair of jeans while Pandimora wore a half buttoned dress shirt of his that landed at her knees. He frowned, trying to remember. After the tub, they'd gone back into the bedroom and snuggled under the bedcovers where sometime during the night they'd made love again, but this time it had been slow and sensual as they'd explored more about each other's body.

They both stood, steadying each other. Bemused, he looked around again. "Drew," she began hesitantly, staring up at the ceiling. "Somehow we have been transported --"

"Yeah."

" -- but I'm not sure where."

He too looked up at the stone ceiling. "Another dimension?" He cleared his throat. "We're in an underground cavern."

Pandimora gripped his hand tightly, her expression perplexed. "Could this be the cavern in my dream?" Her voice rose in excitement.

"Are you serious?" he asked, curious despite himself. The cavern had a muted light but he had no idea the source. Across from them was a high, narrow passageway in the rock in the shape of an inverted teardrop. Deep in the opening was more light. Was that a way out? "How did we get here?" he asked.

Pandimora began to make her way down across jagged rocks to a fairly level, sandy area below them. "Drew, this may be the opportunity I've been seeking all along. If we can find the missing crystal, I can finally get answers about my family. From the basic history I do know of Aisywel, this may be the last known location of the crystal."

He looked at her, shocked. "We're in your faerie world Aisywel?"

"No. I believe we're somewhere below the earth's surface, which in itself is relevant to Aisywel's history. I believe we were propelled here due to the energy of my dream."

"But how did you actually know to come here?" he asked, concerned.

"Irfin told me in the dream."

"Irfin?" That gave Drew a bad feeling. "I'm not sure that's a great idea, to be following anything Irfin says." In fact, he thought it was a really bad idea to trust Irfin at all.

She put a hand out to him. "I'm sorry you've been brought here. Something has gone awry."

"Somehow, I'm not surprised," he said, still thinking of Irfin's involvement. "Does this mean you teleported involuntarily?"

"It's never occurred before. I have always consciously directed myself where I wished to go." She looked up at the cathedral ceiling, a sense of wonder on her face. "I have no explanation as to how we slipped through dimensions."

Drew looked around warily. "Is there any chance we'll encounter goblins or anything?"

"Why would they come here? There is nothing here for them. Besides, there is a law of order, Drew. Lower realms don't pass into the higher realms."

"Well, apparently not everything abides by the rules," he pointed out. "You went to the goblins for help shifting into Aisywel, and Isidghe is lower than earth, but goblins are granted access to earth."

"That's true, but there's a special verbal agreement in place that allows goblins access to the earth only at specified times."

"You're kidding, right? Based on what I've read about goblins, they're a pretty lawless bunch. Are you going to tell me they never violate the agreement?" He gingerly followed her down across the rocks. The jagged edges bit into his feet since he was not used to going without shoes or boots. "Don't tell me," he added, "Goblins are granted access so they can scare the crap out of humans."

She looked at him over her shoulder, nodding with a slight grin. "On special occasions such as Halloween."

Pandimora had already reached the sandy area about six feet below, touching the stones, pausing, as if she were listening to something. Slowly, she climbed up the rocks on the other side to a long rectangular and upraised stone slab. Uneasily, Drew thought it looked like some kind of ceremonial table. The slab itself was surrounded by sandy ground.

"Why are the goblins allowed into our world?"

he asked.

"A long time ago, the goblins were enlisted to keep more ferocious spirits from terrorizing the earth. What you would call demons. In return, they were allowed days of fun as long as they kept the demons away."

"Are there still demons?"

"They are mostly under control. So you see, the goblins do your race a big service."

"I'll take your word for it," Drew said. "I don't know if I'll ever get used to any of this lurking under what I used to think was a normal life."

Sweat beaded on his chest as the air grew even warmer. As he tried to decipher some thinly drawn pictures on the tall ceiling, the rock appeared to waver. He blinked sweat from his eyes. "Pandimora, the heat is rising. And do you hear that sound?" he added, uneasy. "Like a rumble under the ground." As he climbed to where she stood, the noise grew closer.

"It sounds like it's coming from under our feet," he said.

The ground trembled and they heard a muted boom. From behind a large grouping of rocks about thirty feet away, flames suddenly shot into the air.

"Get down!" Drew said. They dropped to the ground. Drew rolled, taking her with him as bits of rock spewed from the flames. The sound was deafening and the ground tremors were disconcerting. It reminded him of an earthquake he'd experienced while living on the west coast.

Quickly, they scooted backwards from the bits of flaming debris. "Come on," he said urgently, "let's get behind the stone slab." He heaved himself onto the slab and dropped down the other side. "There's a cavity here that might offer protection." He held his hand out to her. "Pandimora!"

She scrambled down into the depression and they waited just in case another eruption occurred, but after several moments everything stayed calm.

"That sounded almost like a gas explosion," he said. "Maybe there's gas pockets brewing in the stone under us."

Pandimora stood and leaned over the stone slab, offering a great view of her trim legs and behind. "I need to decipher the writing," she said.

Drew watched as she moved her fingertips across strange lettering chiseled into the stone surface, her brow furrowed in deep concentration. "I must listen to the rocks so that I may find their story." Pandimora closed her eyes and became very still. Patiently, Drew waited, remaining vigilant for other disturbances. Thankfully the ground tremors had ceased, but he remained uneasy nonetheless.

In the quiet, the wind began to wail through a cavern above them. He looked up at the stone formations that looked like thick icicles hanging from the ceiling. Most of them were reddish in color, but there were others that were a beautiful clear crystal.

When Pandimora finally opened her eyes, he saw her acute disappointment. "There was no information about my family," she said. "However, there is information about the crystal." She pressed her lips together. "The crystal lost to time is close," she added in a whisper.

"Here?" he said, astonished. "If you find it, how will you hide it from the elder? Don't you think he's going to want it? I have a bad feeling about this."

"Of course he will want it, but you should know the crystal is very powerful by itself. It's been waiting patiently to be found."

"We have to be quick, Pandimora. I don't know about you, but the heat is making it difficult to breathe." Pandimora's hair, damp with sweat, had begun to curl near her temples, but she seemed otherwise oblivious to the heat as she began to dig, scooping the fine sand with her palms.

"Pandimora, your fingers are bleeding."

"I bleed in the earth realm," she said simply.

"Wipe your fingers on the shirt tails," he said. "Here, let me help you." He gently moved her aside and he began to scoop sand until he hit stones and larger rocks. He dug them out but the sand fell into the cavity left behind. "This might be a losing battle," he muttered. "Are you sure there's something here?"

Carefully, Drew lifted a stone as large as a bowling ball and rolled it away from them and managed to scoop the sand away before it filled the hole.

Pandimora reached down into the pocket and slowly worked free a thin white rod. Carefully, she wiped debris from its surface, but she began to shake her head. "This is not the true crystal," she said, clearly disappointed. "I would feel its power."

Drew watched as the crystal caught the light in the cave and projected it back against the rock. "It's still beautiful," he said. "But it's like it was buried there on purpose. Maybe as a decoy?"

She shrugged. "That could be, to draw attention away from the real crystal and discourage those less scrupulous." She came to her feet and looked around.

"What about that opening?" he asked. "It appears to be a passageway."

Pandimora closed her eyes again and quickly reopened them. "Perhaps," she said.

Drew helped her over the rubble of rock and together they went back down to the flat sandy area. A small stretch of shallow water had to be traversed to reach the passage opening. Drew stared at the water in concern. It appeared crystal clear, but he was learning fast that things were not always as they appeared. When Pandimora moved without hesitation toward the water, he quickly grabbed her arm just as she sank up to her knees. Drew pulled her back to him when she managed to get her feet free.

He went back to the rock rubble and picked up a rock the size of a baseball. He dropped it into the shallow water. The rock instantly disappeared, even though the water appeared shallow.

"It's some kind of quicksand," he said grimly. "We have to find another way in." However, the quicksand pool blocked the entire entrance. He looked up at the walls and toward the ceiling.

"The only other way is possibly to grab onto those rock formations hanging from the cavern ceiling." He looked at her. "Are you sure this is the way we have to go, into that opening?"

"For whatever reason, I feel it pulling me."

Pandimora began to pick her way along the

place as she tried to peer into a small crevice between the pillars.

"Can you see anything? It's pretty dark in there." Then he remembered she could see in the dark. As she shifted around, Drew became aware of a new energy pulsing around them.

"Do you feel that?" He peered around them, and the walls seemed to be closing in. Was it his imagination or was he getting claustrophobic?

"The pillars are moving," Pandimora said. In the next moment, a thin gold beam of light shot past her.

"What's that?" he asked, alarmed.

"Drew, reach your hand into the crevice past my shoulder," she said. "Follow the beam of light. See if you feel a crystal."

Drew moved up against Pandimora, reaching his hand into the space where the beam seemed to originate. Pandimora remained with her hands on the crystal pillars and now they seemed to also be gently pulsing.

He moved his hand around until he felt a warm rod-like shape protruding from the cool stone wall. "It feels like it's attached to the wall."

"I'm going to move out of your way without losing contact with the crystal pillars." She crouched down and looked up at him. "Reach in and pull it out straight toward you."

Drew closed his hand around the crystal rod. "What if it breaks?" he asked, blinking as sweat ran into his eyes.

"It won't break unless it wants to," she said reassuringly.

Drew put all his strength into pulling the crystal

free, his own momentum sending him backwards on the sandy ground. Smaller crystal stalactites rained down on his head. He looked at the crystal in his hand. The cloudy white crystal was about four inches long and perhaps an inch thick, he felt the powerful vibrations traveling from the crystal into his body. Thousands of light prisms swirled pinpoints of color along the crystal enshrouded walls. Mesmerized, he watched the light bounce.

Almost dazed by its power, he held the crystal out to Pandimora.

She dropped her hands from the pillars and came to her feet. As she took the crystal, a flash of white light snapped between them.

He blinked.

"Pandimora!"

She was gone. There was nowhere she could have gone without walking past him, but she'd just disappeared into thin air.

Drew ran down the passage way and back out to the cavern, calling her name.

No answer.

He ran back to the crystal pillars. Taking a deep breath, knowing Pandimora could be in deep trouble, he ducked his head and stepped between them.

Nothing.

A blurred picture formed before him in the air, about waist high, then it came into sharp focus. A small red-headed child ran forward, a toy lamb clutched to her chest. She wore an old fashioned blue dress with white dots to her knees and a cream-colored apron over the dress. Her legs and feet were bare. The lamb came alive, wriggled in the child's arms, and jumped to the ground. With a delighted giggle, the little girl ran after it as it cavorted through a small cottage, jumping over furniture before it disappeared under a small trundle bed.

The little girl went down on her knees to retrieve the lamb but a woman carrying an infant entered the room behind her, took her by the arm, urging her to her feet. The woman's movements were jerky, her eyes red and swollen; her hair as deeply red as the child's but pulled outward in wild, crazy abandon. She hustled the child across the small cottage.

The little girl's happy expression changed, her big blue eyes welling with tears as the older woman opened a floor-to-ceiling cupboard and motioned the child inside. The woman hesitated a moment, then she placed the swaddled infant in the child's arms. "Pandimora, protect your sister as I protect you now. I love you, my dear ones." The woman's voice sounded far away, muffled. Drew saw a star appear on Pandimora's arm and a triple spiral appear on the infant's shoulder.

The woman closed the door and chanted something unintelligible, then turned to a dark-haired young man of about sixteen who came up behind her.

"Mother!" said the young man, "are you crazy? Release the children from the cupboard!"

"Kirklas. It is too late. Too late." The woman thrust her hand and the young man Kirklas clutched his arm protectively to his chest, looking at her with disbelief. Pushing up his long black sleeve, he exposed his arm, bloodied from wrist to shoulder. The betrayal in his eyes was clear as he stumbled back, reaching to catch himself before he fell.

"There was never a choice!" the woman cried. "All this time, never a choice!" She spun around, her eyes wild as she ran out the cottage door. The young man looked dazed and tried to reach the cupboard door again, but he dissolved into thin air before he could do so.

The image slowly faded and Drew let out the breath he'd been holding. Feeling lightheaded, he leaned against one of the pillars.

A hologram of Pandimora, her sister and brother Kirklas. Confused, Drew wondered what this was all about. And where was Pandimora?

∞ Chapter Ten ∞

"I believe you have something that belongs to me." Lukais' deep voice jerked Pandimora into full alertness. Adrenalin surging, she quickly looked for Drew but found herself alone. He had not transported with her. She held her fear in check. What had gone wrong? Was he all right?

"Do not look for the human. I pulled you from the crystal cave. Of what use is he to me?"

She stiffened, lying on her side on Drew's bed, the covers crumpled around her. Her hand holding the crystal lay underneath her. Lukais stood about ten feet in front of her. Somehow Lukais already knew she'd found the crystal.

The elder appeared surrounded by a hazy aura, as if in a tumultuous state standing here in the earth realm. Pandimora blinked several times, puzzled by how out of focus everything appeared.

"You are fully ensnared by the human," Lukais

remarked with derision. "And you do not seem to care Aisywel is thrown into chaos due to your continued rebellion." He put up a slender hand. "I understand, Pandimora. I myself felt such romantic pangs in my younger years. But the humans are too different from us. They will only bring you anguish and betrayal as you will discover in time."

Pandimora studied the elder curiously, the white hair neatly flowing back from his wide forehead, just touching his shoulders. His pale blue eyes pierced, making her want to squirm, but she resisted. She reminded herself of what he had done. All the time she had grown up she'd felt him to be a mentor, caring for she and her sister. But all that had been turned upside down the day she fled Aisywel, fearing for her immortality.

"That is your history with a human," she said softly. "Not mine." She didn't want it to be hers.

She created clothing to cover her body from his gaze. While faeries felt no shame or embarrassment about the body, some part of her deep inside wished to conceal from Lukais' gaze not only the physical body she had shared with Drew, but also her true light form. She fretted over Drew, wondered if he was still stuck in the cavern. She couldn't recall anything beyond standing within the crystal pillars as Drew handed her the crystal, and then awakening here.

"If you once loved a human, Lukais, then you understand how compelling such a relationship can be," she said now, trying to stall for time. Part of her wondered if the failure of his relationship with a human had removed all vestiges of sympathy for their race. The crystal grew hot in her palm. She knew he wanted it.

"The earth plane will never sustain you, Pandimora. You are a creature of the fae, no matter your lineage. You will never be happy with such a boring, pallid existence. Come back to us and forget all that has gone before."

"I can't," she remarked stonily, surprised she no longer felt shaky under his penetrating stare. "You have created great disharmony with your deeds. It is you, not I."

"Your tongue has grown sharp while you have been away, and your words are most disrespectful. The crystal belongs in my care. I must have it now."

She tightened her hand around the crystal rod, wondering how she'd keep him from taking it.

He lifted his dark eyebrows, waiting.

Pandimora sat up, the crystal still behind her.

Lukais gave a slight sigh and imperiously held out his hand.

She used every bit of power she possessed to resist, but her hand lifted towards him nonetheless. His brows came together in anger. "I am through with your defiance, Pandimora. You will obey me as your high elder."

Pandimora looked down and instead of the clear beauty of the crystal, in her hand was a nubby brown stick. She tightened her fingers around it in surprise. In truth she didn't know where the crystal had gone. She held tightly to the stick, silently thanking it for substituting itself for that of the crystal.

"If you had requested I give you the crystal wand

before all this mistrust I would simply have handed it to you," she said. "But I doubt your sincerity."

He looked taken aback, but quickly recovered. "It is blasphemous, Pandimora, for you to question my decisions and intentions. You have lived your entire life in serenity and play thanks to my calming authority over the worlds. Why suddenly throw away that which you have known your entire life?"

"I have not turned my back on my beloved Aisywel," she declared passionately. "But I'm not like you, Lukais. I have not hidden away anyone's family. I have not struck down another faerie."

"I have not taken your family," he said, but his voice seemed stiff to her. "It is clear you care more for the humans."

"I care for both worlds," she said defiantly. "You exiled me from my home." Intense pain slipped through her guard. "You took my memories."

"You saw with your eyes Clare was out of control."

"Perhaps all I saw was a limited version of what occurred. You have control over the crystal."

"You were shown the truth of that time long past." He touched the silver amulet suspended on a fine chain from his neck. It winked at her mesmerizingly, but after a brief glance Pandimora kept her gaze away from it. She would not be mind washed and she feared he would use any means to subdue her.

"Our world is at a crossroads, Pandimora. If you choose not to cooperate, I will have no choice but to suspend you in the space between dimensions until you go before the elder high council." His presence became more imposing, but Pandimora made herself remain still.

"If you were meant to have the crystal, it would have been allowed," she said defiantly, and she quickly leapt from the bed and ran out into the living room.

Pandimora flinched at the deep roar behind her. It reached higher than the heavens and stronger than any known human sound. She was grateful Drew was not present because it might have ruptured his human ears.

She searched the counter top for the protective device Irfin had given her, but it was gone. She turned her back to the counter, its hard surface pressing against her spine as the elder advanced. Nervously, she pinched her wrist and looked down at her unmarred skin in surprise. It was then she realized the elder had invaded her dream. She pinched again and again, but she could not surface from her dream.

***

"Pandimora!" Drew's own voice startled him. He was back in his home. He untangled his feet from the twisted bed sheets and jumped off the bed to hurry into the adjoining bath. "Pandimora!" He turned back and rushed through his bedroom, confused to see he was back in his boxer shorts. He ran out to the kitchen and the hallway and pulled open the front door. A blast of icy wind hit his chest. Everything was blotted white outside. He pushed the door closed with his foot and walked into the dimly lit living room. Had all this been some warped dream or was he losing his mind?

He swung his head back and forth, looking, searching for her. His heart beat furiously as he suddenly saw her lying on the living room couch, her arms and legs moving slightly, twitching in sleep.

He hurried over to her, staring down at her, her luxurious hair draped across one shoulder. Gently, he covered her with a light blue throw but turned quickly when the front door opened and an icy gust blew inside, snow landing in puffs on his entryway tiles.

Drew stepped over to the bookcase beside him and grabbed the baseball bat he kept there. Irfin suddenly put his head around the door then thrust his hands into the air. "Here now, put that away," he said, out of breath. "I've come to warn you it's Him who's on his way."

Drew let the bat rest on the floor beside him. "Close the door."

"Doesn't really matter. Listen and don't ask questions. I've popped into your dream. You're both still asleep, but this is no natural sleep. Himself is searching for the crystal so he's cast an enchantment to keep you dreaming."

"How do you know?"

"Because I'm not dreaming," Irfin declared, exasperated.

"I don't know if I can trust you. Your protection device didn't work on the goblins and you said it would protect us."

"Not for goblins," Irfin said.

"What's up with you Irfin?" Drew advanced on the little man. "Did someone promise you something

-- immortality for your wife? Is that the price for betraying Pandimora?"

Irfin gave a high-pitched whistle and Drew put his hands over his ears. Irfin slammed the front door, his face red. "We don't have time for chit chat. You're dreaming and you have to listen to me."

"Why would I believe you?"

"I'm monitoring your brain waves. He needs you to remain asleep so he can move in and out while he searches."

"So does that mean you're sleeping too?"

"No," Irfin said impatiently. "I've jumped into your dream. Both of you need to wake up. We have work to do."

"So you're waking us up inside a dream?" Drew muttered, feeling incredibly dense.

"Something like that. We don't have time for a detailed explanation."

"What work?"

"You have to get rid of the elder."

"Get rid of him now?" Drew asked warily, moving to kneel beside Pandimora. He put the back of his hand gently against her cheek.

"Take him out of commission until we can figure out how to safeguard the crystal."

"So you know about that, too?"

"Yes. I know everything that's happened since you left this realm."

Drew looked at him quickly.

"Well, almost everything," Irfin muttered, his face now red. "I'm not a peeping Tom. I knew Pandimora was the only one who could find the crystal, given her special gift. All this time the crystal patiently waited for her to find it."

Irfin stared at the crystal still clutched in Pandimora's hand. It glowed with a surreal light against the dark blue fabric of the couch cushions. She moved restlessly but did not awaken.

"Pandimora," Drew said urgently, gently shaking her shoulder. "Pandimora. Wake up."

"You can't wake her from a dream while you're dreaming. First you have to wake up yourself."

"How the heck do I do that?" Drew demanded. "Why don't you wake me up?"

"I can do it remotely," Irfin finally said, "but you might not like it."

"Just do it."

***

"Why didn't you tell me you were going to give me an electric jolt?" Drew demanded. He felt like he'd just been plugged into the electric grid.

"Time's getting short and you said just do it." Irfin said.

"Something I'll never say to you again," Drew said shortly. "What did you do, taser me?"

"Of course not," Irfin said. "But I did give you a wee jolt of electricity. It was the quickest way to pull you from the trance."

"Well, you're not doing that to Pandimora." Drew stood protectively in front of the couch.

"We might not have a choice," muttered Irfin, moving closer to where she lay. "You have to change her body temperature in some way or create a jolt, such as the one I gave you."

Drew put out his hand. "No. Just wait. Let me do it my way."

He hurried into his bathroom and put a clean washcloth under the faucet, then ran it under cold water. He came back out and knelt beside her, putting the cold washcloth on her forehead and cheeks, but she remained unmoving. He looked up at Irfin. "What about ice cubes?"

Drew hurried into the kitchen, shaking ice cubes from the freezer trays. He dumped them on the counter and grabbed half a dozen cubes. Returning to Pandimora, he put them in the washcloth and put it against the tender skin of her neck. He was thankful when she began to stir and finally awoke. He sat back on his heels when she sat up, frowning, obviously groggy.

She clutched the crystal to her breasts with both hands. "Lukais tried to take the crystal," she said. "I was dreaming but I was deeply submerged and couldn't get out."

Drew brought her up to speed on what had happened while Irfin impatiently paced back and forth. "The good news is you found the crystal," Irfin said.

She nodded. "It was so strange. We teleported without direction into the crystal cavern."

"Not really. You were both dreaming," Irfin declared. "How else would you teleport together while asleep?" He bit his lip. "This is most unusual, for a human to be teleported in the dream phase with a faerie. Most unusual indeed." His eyes began to brighten. "However, the good news is the crystal if safe and sound. The not so good news is the crystal rightfully belongs to Lukais as supreme power and be assured he intends to take it."

"No." Drew rejected that immediately.

Pandimora clenched her jaw. "I'm not turning it over to him. You have no idea what he has planned. He will decimate all worlds," she cried, panic in her voice.

"You will have no choice," Irfin stated. "How do you propose to keep evading him?"

"After all this you can't be serious," Drew said.

"He will return. Once he has the crystal, we will know then if he can be trusted or not."

"That'll be helpful," Drew said sarcastically. "He can obliterate us and we'll die knowing he's the bad guy."

Irfin drew himself to his full height, his expression fierce. "The elder does what he feels is necessary to protect the world of the fae. All any of us can do is what our conscience will allow."

"Well, that's pretty convenient," Drew said sarcastically. "So you are on his side?" He looked at Pandimora. "I had a feeling we couldn't trust him."

Irfin rolled his eyes. "I'm looking at the entire picture and all the probabilities. There really is no right or wrong, just outcomes."

"I'm looking at it from a human perspective," Drew said. "If he abuses his power, faeries disappear. Humans too. You can't condone it."

"How long do we have before he finds us?" Pandimora asked urgently.

"We are on borrowed time now. I need the crystal, and your masking devices as they're calibrated to your individual frequencies. Right now, it's the best I can do." Irfin held his hand out to Pandimora. She hesitated, stared at him a moment, then reluctantly handed him the crystal. Irfin accepted it almost reverently, then stared at it fixedly, his short, thick fingers stroking down one smooth side.

"The masking devices are on the kitchen counter. Why do you need the crystal?" Drew asked, uneasy to see it leave Pandimora's hand.

"To protect it," Irfin muttered. "To make sure it ends up where it belongs." As Drew watched the air around Irfin began to blur and move in waves, as if the little man was part of a puzzle being pulled apart.

He watched in horror as the man snapped the crystal in two. Hardly able to believe his eyes, he stared at the jagged edges then up at Irfin.

"No!" Pandimora's scream barely registered as they both lunged toward the little man.

"It's for the best!" Irfin shouted, then he dropped into a portal that materialized in the floor. "Get your devices! The elder is approaching fast. None of us are safe."

Drew tried to grab him but Irfin was gone. Frantically, he pushed at the wood floor which was once again solid. Grimly, Drew looked at Pandimora. "Gone -- with the crystal. Open a portal --"

"I can't." For the first time he heard desperation in her voice. "I have no energy flow to do so."

"Has all this been one big plan for Irfin to snatch the crystal?"

"No," she said staunchly. "No. He would not betray his own."

Drew paced the floor. "What are his loyalties? He's been planning this from the start. He's got to be in league with the elder. He was probably promised immortality for his wife. I don't think it really matters to him who gets hurt."

Pandimora stared at him. "What are you talking about?"

Drew told her what he knew from his investigation for Irfin's wife.

She shook her head. "I knew he had family in both realms. No, I will not believe Irfin is in league with Lukais."

He stared at her. "Maybe he's not."

"But you just said --"

"Maybe he's in this for himself alone. Maybe he's selling the crystal to the highest bidder? Or maybe he's got plans of his own for the crystal and will harness its power or something. What do you really know about him, except that he conveniently showed up when you were in crisis? Had you ever met him before?"

Doubtfully, Pandimora shook her head no.

"Maybe he waited just out of sight that night I found you. I know I saw something or someone hiding on the side of the road. Could he have been planning this all along? Did Lukais put him up to it?" Drew knelt beside her. "We have to go after Irfin and recover the crystal."

She nodded, her face troubled. She bit her lip. "I wonder now ..."

"What?"

"All the time we were in the crystal cavern, it was all within my dream. Irfin knew, as did the elder."

"And if Irfin's telling the truth, you're the only

one empowered to retrieve the crystal. Meanwhile, they just waited for your return to snatch it. We can't trust them, you must see that now." He stared at her hard, ready to argue the point if she still disagreed. However, seeing the crushed look on her face, the expression of being betrayed, he put his arms around her. "I will protect you," he vowed. "We'll figure this out."

The explosion wrenched them apart.

∞ Chapter Eleven ∞

Pandimora crawled on her knees to where Drew lay motionless in the destruction of his living room. Carefully, she removed a beam and pieces of the ceiling from across his chest. Breathing hard, her panic escalated when he remained unmoving. She could see a deep purpling began under his ribs and extend up into his chest area. She pushed back the tears. Could he be hurt inside, his organs crushed?

"Drew?" she touched his pale cheek but there was no response. Closing her eyes, she concentrated on the beat of his heart. Distressed, she bit back a cry. She could feel his life force ebbing and knew he was close to death.

She looked around wildly, not certain what had caused the explosion or even if there was still a threat. Something had rocked the house apart and now there was absolute silence as the snow fell on them from a hole in the roof, coating everything in white. She expected to see the elder arrive at any moment, yet a stillness hung around them. The elder wanted to kill Drew, knowing how much he meant to her. She bit her lips to keep from crying.

Drew's skin began to take on a frightening gray tinge. He needed immediate care. A human hospital? No, instinct told her he would die by the time he got there. That left the healing sanctuary, but was it safe? Sometimes humans did not react favorably to faerie healing. She also knew there was only one chance. If it failed, he would surely die.

She tried to materialize a portal. Frustrated, she tried again but nothing happened. Her entire life she'd known how to conjure a portal in any dimension but something was terribly wrong. Had Irfin taken everything from them or was it the elder working magic from the faerie realm?

Pandimora ran into the bedroom and pulled a blanket off the bed to cover Drew, then she quickly moved into the kitchen, but the devices that had been on the counter were gone. She hadn't seen Irfin take them earlier, even though he'd asked about them. She ran her hand over the smooth counter top then realized the explosion had bounced them into the sink. She grabbed both devices with relief and ran back to Drew. The tremors shaking his body frightened her.

"Drew. I need to get you to a safe place, but I can't conjure a portal and I'm afraid you'll die if you stay here. Tell me what to do in your world." He remained unresponsive. Carefully, she tucked the blanket around him, placed her body over his without putting weight on him, and with a device in each hand, closed her eyes and squeezed the discs.

When she opened her eyes they were at Dell's Bridge, the snow swirling madly around them. She closed her eyes and squeezed the discs again, concentrating on gaining entry to the sanctuary.

Pandimora opened her eyes to a warm, gentle wind. Several small faeries lifted Drew weightlessly and carried him with them. Pandimora ran after them as they whisked him through amber-lit shadows, golden light spilling down as they moved to an open pool of water. Pandimora clenched her fists agitatedly, hoping they were in time. She couldn't lose him. Had it taken this terrible event where he hovered near death, for her to realize how she felt about him? She bit her fist. She couldn't lose him now!

The faeries suspended Drew on his back in the healing waters, a pool with white curls of electricity along its surface, moving to enclose Drew in a protective embrace. His strongly muscled arms and legs did not move, nor did his eyes open. Pandimora held her breath, waiting for a sign that he was still alive. The purpled skin was now almost black across his chest. His fingertips, toes and lips were a frightening shade of blue.

The faeries moved past her, dusting the moss-covered ground with faerie dust. Pandimora realized they were removing Drew's scent from the ground he had passed over.

"Will he be safe here?" she asked anxiously, looking around the beautiful forest and into the shadows. Could there be danger lurking even in this peaceful sanctuary?

The smallest faerie looked up from her task, her short blonde hair falling into her sparkling eyes. "There is nothing else you can do," she said, her voice sympathetic but firm. "If anything can save him, it will be this. Let the waters weave their magic."

As she stared at Drew, Pandimora felt torn. She didn't want to leave him but she knew the crystal had to be recovered. Aisywel and, indeed, all dimensions could be at risk with Irfin having taken it. If he gave it to the elder, all would be lost. Pandimora shivered with fear. She'd seen the future the elder envisioned.

She hated to admit it, but Drew might be right about Irfin being involved with the elder. How had she thought Irfin sincere? Had the elder and Irfin set her and Drew up to retrieve the crystal and had now decided their usefulness was at an end?

Pandimora sank down to the mossy ground as deep blue twilight fell over the sanctuary. A rich essence of nurturing souls flitted around her. Beautiful twinkling stars shone overhead, and a warm breeze caressed her cheeks. The sanctuary emulated Aisywel so well that an intense wave of homesickness hit Pandimora. She thought of the loss of her family, her home and her identity. How had she thought she, a lone faerie, could ever find the truth held by beings far superior in strength and age? She felt no nearer the truth than when she'd first been ousted from her dear home.

And now Drew, a mortal who held her heart in his hands, teetered on the brink of death. How had she thought she could become involved with him and then leave?

There was a thin line for a human between survival and letting go as a body system deteriorated, the blood stopped supplying life to major organs, and the body shut down. The thought of losing Drew doubled her over with the pain. Pandimora tried to catch her breath, but emotions and thoughts she had never experienced before hit her squarely between the eyes. As trees lovingly formed an umbrella around her, she wept, the sobs wrenching and deep, incapacitating her as full realization embedded itself: she stood on the verge of losing everything she'd thought was hers to love. She cried tears for the familial love she could have had, for the loss of loving arms, and for the small child she'd been, and lastly for the memories that had been stolen away.

When eventually the storm of emotion abated, Pandimora slowly became cognizant of her surroundings, the tree now against her back, the light ever changing from twilight to dawn, twilight and dawn again. Where did a faerie go to find answers no longer available? As rich gilded light crept under the tree's sheltering limbs, Pandimora stretched her legs, the sun's golden light bathing her in its warm, healing rays. Somehow, she felt the filtering of a new strength within and she had to wonder if this sanctuary also healed emotions of loss and despair.

Taking a slow, measured breath, Pandimora came to her feet. She had a choice to make. Stay here with Drew or continue the search for the crystal. It was no longer just her longing to know the truth about her family; it now involved the lives of all living beings. And the heartbreaking truth was Drew would be safer if she was not in his life.

She looked toward Drew, the waters holding him now an effervescent bubbling green. His skin no longer had the horrible gray tinge but his condition still scared her. He could easily die, even in this beautiful sanctuary.

"Goodbye, Drew."

***

Pandimora's search led her through inter-dimensions that were empty of life. She felt as if she followed an old trail, and she concentrated deeply, seeing more dimensions in her mind's eye than even she knew existed. Tentatively, she pressed through another dimension and felt a soul vibrating within.

"You're here," Irfin's voice came flatly from behind her, and the words were accompanied by a sigh.

Pandimora quickly turned. "Did you think I'd just let you leave?"

"I knew you wouldn't understand," the little man said. He sat perched atop a stump that glowed in colors of pale peach. "You're angry about the crystals. No harm was ever meant to you or Drew. I was not responsible for the explosion. I tried to avert it, but Lukais had already set it in motion. I warned you to grab the devices," he added, not quite meeting her eyes.

"Why, Irfin?" she asked.

"I felt you'd be safe if I sent you through your dreams to find the crystal. There was less risk that way."

She clenched her fists. "Now I truly understand the emotions related to feeling betrayed. How could you do this?"

But he did not reply.

Pandimora paced the smooth ground, the surroundings bland and lacking life. "You sent us to secure it and then you steal it with no explanation." Despite trying to remain calm, Pandimora knew her raised voice carried traces of aggression as it echoed all around them.

"I'm gratified you are not afraid of stating your opinion," he said. "I thought about telling you I needed the crystal, but I couldn't risk it. If Lukais had pulled the information from you prematurely, all would have been lost."

"Why?"

"The crystal belongs to the fae."

"I agree, but this was not the way to do it! And now you have destroyed the crystal by snapping it in two!" Pandimora said. "Surely its power is diminished?"

"On the contrary," Irfin exclaimed, holding up two crystals. "We now have twice the crystal power." Pandimora stared at the crystals, equally beautiful, both four inches or longer. "I tested my theory that I might be able to grow the crystals. Aren't they magnificent?" he asked with glee, moving the crystals this way and that so the light caught them, spinning all the colors of the light spectrum in the air around them.

Pandimora couldn't shake the feeling she'd been betrayed. "Drew was right, you planned this from the start -- my ejection from Aisywel, you pulling

Drew into this scheme and then taking the crystal for your own means."

"It was not that simple Pandimora." He placed the crystals out of sight in a pocket. "I never meant to put you or Drew in harm's way."

"What did you think would happen when the elder found out the crystal was found? Of course there would be repercussions! And here you sit, still intent on keeping the crystals."

"The machinations set in place were unavoidable. These crystals must be returned to Aisywel," he said stubbornly.

"'To Lukais."

"It is one and the same," he said. "They should never have been separated."

"Who hid the crystal?"

He shrugged. "Who is to know?"

Pandimora turned away impatiently. "You have betrayed me and more importantly you have betrayed who you are. Drew hovers near death -- how can I dare to hope he will live and how will I ever find my family now? The elder cannot be trusted and it appears neither can you."

Quietly, Irfin said, "Pandimora, choices had to be made -- however, rest your mind, your sister has left Aisywel for the moment and is in the earth dimension."

For the first time since leaving Aisywel, Pandimora felt a moment's relief. Her sister was safe.

"But it appears there are already stirrings of trouble," Irfin continued, "since it is reported the portals have been locked."

Pandimora's worst fears began to materialize. "Locked?"

"Due to the manifesting unrest, the dark creatures in the netherworld are stirring. I've even heard they're clamoring at the portals."

"So faerie and human alike may suffer. Lukais will make innocent blood flow through Aisywel because of his stubbornness, his determination to hold his insane plan to harness the crystal power for his own ends. And you will be by his side." Pandimora swung away from him, shaking with helpless anger. "I have been a fool to trust in the goodness of the fae. When did all this turn around? How could I not see it, the evil lurking all around me?"

"Pandimora, you are upset and concerned about the future of dear Aisywel, as am I. It is a terrible thing that Drew got caught in the crossfire of our dimensions. I am doing my best to lay the plans for the future, but it is impossible to promise lives will not be lost."

"What if I had failed to find the crystal?"

Irfin smiled gently. "Pandimora, you have a great soul gift, destined to create world change with your talents and your ability to care. You were chosen for this specific purpose because I knew you could be trusted to do what is right."

"And what about you, Irfin? Will you do what is right?"

"I will do what I must." Irfin avoided her eyes, looked instead at a device on his wrist. "Come with me. I can renegotiate your return to Aisywel."

She shook her head, backing away. "No. I need to

recover my family."

"Clare and Declan are gone, Pandimora," he said quietly.

Pandimora drew in a quick breath, and another. "I will not lose what I had always wished to have."

"They chose their path so that their children may live."

She could barely breathe. "What are you talking about?"

"They let their souls be burned into the afterlife so their children could survive. It was an agreement."

"An agreement? How do you know this?" she asked suspiciously.

He sighed. "You are not the only one who has heard the elder's thoughts."

"So he is responsible for their banishment?"

"I don't know. All I know is he is aware there was a signed agreement that night."

Stubbornly, she shook her head. "I will find them."

"Pandimora!"

She ran, pushing herself from the dimension. Panic burned through her. She must return to Isidghe and convince the goblins to help her shift matter. Her parents could not be gone. She would find them.

It was time she returned to Aisywel, but on her own terms.

∞ Chapter Twelve ∞

Pandimora summoned the goblins to her as she stood just on the outer edge of the earth realm. Using her sweetest voice, the one that exposed the truth in her heart, she promised to bargain with them for their help.

Jonic materialized first, grinning with his stubby brown teeth, and Sirt appeared next, one eyebrow cocked as he stared at her. They both appeared delighted to realize they were very close to the earth dimension and tilted their heads back to eagerly sniff the air.

"You have not brought the human," Jonic said with disappointment, and yet she noted his eyes shone with delight, no doubt for the mischief he hoped to create. At least he was honest in his dealings with her.

Sirt nudged Jonic aside. "You're always thinking of your own enjoyment. She did not call us to frighten her human." He turned to her. "Why have you called us so close to the earth dimension?"

"I knew it would interest you enough to answer my summons," Pandimora stated quietly. "I did not mean to trick you, but Aisywel is falling into ruin as we speak. I need to shift matter so that I might return and speak to the high elder council. There is information I must give them to prepare them for the turmoil that lies ahead. I need your help."

Sirt looked at her, aghast. "In returning you risk stepping into disaster! The ground will be air and the climate will squeeze the breath from your faerie lungs. You cannot return."

Fear sliced through Pandimora, and resolve. "I can and I will. Tell me how to shift matter so I can get in undetected, without the use of a portal. I need to be less than a grain of sand so that I might slip through the other side."

Jonic put his palms together and quickly twiddled his fingers, his glance calculating. "And what will we get in return?" His anticipation was so sharp she could feel it.

Pandimora bit her lip. "We will strike a bargain," she said slowly. "I will ask Drew if he can arrange for you an extra day in the earth dimension."

"The human," remarked Sirt. "But he is not well. He lies dying."

"He will get better," she said fiercely. "He will."

"Well, of course I do hope you are right," Jonic said delicately, "however, if plans change, what else are you willing to bargain?"

"I must act quickly," she said. "Can we discuss this later? I promise I will uphold my end of a bargain."

"You swear?" Sirt asked, eyes narrowed. "On your immortal life?"

Pandimora nodded, aware of the risk she took, promising an open-ended bargain with a goblin.

Jonic took her hand, his fingers clammy. "We'll help an Aisywel faerie and hopefully live to tell about it. You must come to our world as the shift can only be made from Isidghe, just as the return must be to Isidghe. If you try to step into a different dimension, then poof," he blew a gust of air suddenly into her face. "You will be faerie dust. We don't usually do this with faeries, so we can't guarantee your safety when you shift over there."

He looked at Sirt. "Do we need her to sign a disclaimer?"

"Please trust me. I won't hold you responsible if something goes wrong."

"Mmm." Jonic frowned, obviously not at all happy about this turn of events. "Goblins don't like to be rushed, but okay, we'll do it." He pulled a scroll of paper from behind him, held it up and let it unroll to his feet. She stared at it, then watched as he kicked it with his foot and unrolled it the rest of the way.

"I-I --"

Sirt hit Jonic on the shoulder. "Put that away. Can't you see she's in distress? She promised, and unlike goblins, Aisywel faeries don't lie."

Pandimora nodded and took a deep breath.

Jonic started to roll the scroll, but it kinked and the parchment began to crumple. With a sound of frustration, he dropped it to the ground. "All right," he said to Sirt. "But if this goes awry, don't say I didn't warn you."

Sirt indicated the elven star on her arm. "As you shift you must concentrate on the star and invoke its protective qualities. Use all your powers of concentration. We hope doing this will bring you into Aisywel without mishap."

She nodded. "I'm ready."

"One other thing," Jonic snapped. "We're coming with you."

Pandimora had not expected that. "It's very dangerous," she said somberly, but they merely stared at her with barely suppressed anticipation.

"It sounds like great fun," said Jonic. "I can't wait to see the faces of those Aisywel faeries."

***

Pandimora felt her body rebuilding itself, one molecule and cell at a time as she shifted into Aisywel. She concentrated on the protective elven star, afraid at any moment she would turn to dust and all would be lost.

Her heart positioned itself in her chest, beating very hard and fast. She was frightened, but the matter shift appeared to have worked and she was finally back home. As Sirt and Jonic materialized beside her, she motioned for them to follow. She had to be quick to find the high elder council and then she had to make them listen. She paused a moment on the edge of the forest, noting the faeries hurrying toward the hillocks, into the woods, their faces filled with fear and concern. They did not seem to notice her or the goblins. Her senses picked up an unusual sense of urgency and she wondered at the levels of distress evident.

Looking at the goblins she put a finger to her lips. They gave her an odd look. "What's wrong?" she asked.

"You're a bit pale and faded," whispered Sirt. He reached for her hand and looking down, Pandimora was alarmed to see she was somewhat transparent.

"I'd say you're not all here," Jonic remarked.

"Does this usually happen?" she asked.

Jonic shrugged. "Don't know. This is the first time we've shifted matter for a faerie. Hopefully in time the rest of you will arrive." He licked his lips. "Um, it might be a good idea to grasp your arm above the star, as a reminder to invoke its continued protection."

Pandimora did as he suggested, knowing time was precious. "Follow me." She skirted the forest toward the back of the university hall, looking up at the imposing structure, which reached fifteen stories into the sky. Having been away from her beloved Aisywel, she drank in her surroundings as she slipped through the familiar opening in the ancient garden wall. The trees in the garden turned toward her with a soft whisper but then pulled back in alarm as the goblins came into sight. Sirt tried to pull Jonic through the wall but his stomach appeared to be wider than the opening.

Panting, Jonic gasped, "I'll wait here and be a look out. If any faeries come by, I'll be my usual jovial self."

Pandimora looked back at him. "Don't bring attention to yourself," she warned, then bit her lip. Any faerie would know he was a goblin. "Please don't start any mischief."

She stepped into the once beautiful gardens and frowned with dismay. The vegetable garden plots she had so carefully tended had been tilled into the deep rich soil. She felt as if the memory of her existence had been erased also.

A mix of emotions began to simmer; anger, injustice, a sense of helplessness. Angrily, she stepped closer to the back of the university building. Motioning for Sirt to wait, she climbed a small stone wall and leaned against the building, peering through a broken window into the conservatory. It was a prime vantage point for eavesdropping. The leaves growing close to the windows moved aside to make room for her and she pressed closer. Inside the splendid glass hall several members of the elder high council were gathered. Lukais was not present.

Her sensitive ears picked up the thread of conversation. "There is fear and concern among the faeries for the future. Sensing our vulnerability, the netherworld creatures have opened a portal and are flooding Aisywel as we speak. We have arranged a meeting before chaos takes over."

Lukais had implied her rebellion had started the unrest, but how could that be the truth? There must have been trouble before she fled Aisywel.

Pandimora was jerked backwards and she tried to grab the window frame to steady herself. The thin wood splintered, glass spilling over her as she landed on the ground. She looked up at Lukais, fear heavy in her heart.

Sirt and Jonic stood beside Lukais, heavy golden chains of enchantment binding their arms to their bodies and covering their eyes.

She scrambled to her feet. "Let them go. They have done you no harm."

"Pandimora, I cannot believe you have enlisted the aid of -- of goblins! They have broken my law, as have you by being here."

Pandimora looked at him quickly. "Your law or the law of the fae?"

Lukais regarded her dispassionately. "Surely you know it is the same."

"All I have done is seek the truth, yet apparently you consider that to be harmful."

He wove a spell of faerie dust around Pandimora and the goblins. The ground beneath them dissolved and a chasm opened. Fear quivered through every part of her as she felt herself suspended in air.

Pandimora wanted to scream at how helpless she felt. There was nothing solid that she could push or struggle against. In this moment, she virtually did not exist.

"You will not win," she said. "Too many faeries know what you have done," she added brashly, hoping she was right.

He brought his face close to hers and Pandimora averted her eyes from his mesmerizing stare. She wondered if faeries could go mad for surely the glitter in his eyes was troubling. "I will prevail," he said fiercely. "All I have ever done is my duty to ensure no harm comes to Aisywel. I will not step down. I will not give up the crystals."

Pandimora was relieved when he moved away from her, but she knew if he left they would be forgotten for all time. "Release Sirt and Jonic to their world. They are only here because of me. They are innocent in all this. I made them false promises to get them to help me."

He considered the goblins held motionless in their bindings. "I find them harmless enough," he agreed, "although goblins love the scent of chaos and disorder." He added a stern warning to the goblins. "If you return there will be no second chances. Am I understood?" The goblins nodded and quickly suppressed nervous giggles.

To her relief, Lukais waved a hand and the goblins disappeared.

"Your continued interference is going to cost the human. If it's any consolation, he'll never know what hit him. Let this remind you in future you cannot defy me."

Drew. Pandimora held her breath in terror but the elder vanished. Drew. The worst she had feared was happening. She'd thought he'd be safe if she left, but now ...

Alone, suspended in a holding cell with no floor, walls or door, she thought longingly of Drew. She had lost her family, her home ... she couldn't lose him too! She thought it strange that the elder had not asked her about the crystal. Her heart plummeted. That could only mean he already had it, or anticipated having it. Irfin.

The elven star on her arm began to grow warm. Was she to turn into faerie dust? She closed her eyes and put her hand over the star, seeing her mother's face, invoking her protection.

∞ Chapter Thirteen ∞

Drew paced across the mossy ground. He remembered an explosion rocking his house and pain that infiltrated every inch of his body, and then nothing more. When he'd awakened in the healing springs, the faeries had said Pandimora was gone.

He hadn't been able to find a way out of the sanctuary and everyone seemed to have disappeared. At least they'd left him some clothes but he was stuck here until he was teleported out or could find a way out. He didn't see any portals, just this Disney-like setting no matter where he walked.

Where had she gone? Was Pandimora all right?

"Drew, I'm sending help to get you out of there." Drew turned around. Irfin's voice was all around him but he couldn't see him.

"Where are you?" Drew said. "Do you know the mess you've created, the danger you've put Pandimora in? I suppose you've given Lukais the crystal and we're all screwed."

"Calm down --"

"Stop hiding and face me."

"I-I can't -- but I've done the best I can to make this right."

Drew gritted his teeth. "I don't think that's possible."

A hologram began to take shape in front of Drew. He stepped back warily and Irfin's image was before him. Frowning, Drew put his hand through the image. Tiny particles moved around and then reshaped to form Irfin's image once again. "What's going on?"

"This is the best I can do," Irfin said. "Everything's changed in my life."

"I don't care," Drew said harshly. "Where is Pandimora?"

"First, I'm sending someone to get you out. Second, Pandimora is in Aisywel."

"And the elder?"

"Right now he is occupied with lying to the high elder council. Lukais is going to destroy this sanctuary."

"Get me to Pandimora."

Irfin shook his head. "No, your association ends here. You will awaken in your home, which by the way is repaired, and everything will be a hazy dream."

"No. What gives you the right?" Angry, Drew swiped his hand through the hologram, once more displacing the particles. Forget everything? Forget Pandimora?

"Pandimora deserves more than you thinking

you'll love her if she's not sick. She deserves someone who will be there for her no matter what genetics she carries. If you're afraid to love her, she's better off without you."

"This is not up to you." Drew clenched his fists.

"That's right. It's all up to you, Drew." Irfin's image dissolved.

"Irfin -- Irfin -- come back!" Drew felt as if he'd run for miles, his chest suddenly heaving as emotions coursed through him. Forget everything that had happened? He didn't want to forget Pandimora. How do you forget a woman who's never given up on her family, who cares more about doing the right thing than possibly, living? No matter the outcome, he couldn't let her go.

***

Drew kept searching for a way out, but it was like he was the only one here. It appeared even the healing pools had dried up. No portals, no sign of life. Irfin had said the elder would destroy this place but it already looked abandoned as the light faded with each passing moment.

Suddenly, he looked around. Was Irfin back? "Who's there?"

"Goblins," came a gravelly voice behind him.

Drew watched as two beings stepped into the meager light. He saw something that looked like orange crayon outlines walking toward him, then the closer they got they became more solid.

"Geez." He tensed as they solidified and stopped about five feet away. The shorter one gave him a quick head to toe assessment. Drew knew there was nowhere to go.

The creatures were something pulled from a nightmare. The shorter goblin was orange with an enormous stomach. His small bulging purple eyes sat atop a grin that spread from one oversize ear to the next. The second goblin was tall and slim, his blue body covered by pink giraffe-type markings. Drew braced himself, ready to bang some heads together and go down fighting.

The orange goblin turned to the taller blue goblin. "I don't know, Sirt, what do you think? Can we shift him without killing him?"

"You'll have a fight on your hands," Drew said. "Whatever you're thinking about, I'm not going anywhere."

The orange goblin looked disappointed. "You don't want to help Pandimora?"

"What -- where is she?" Drew took a step forward.

"Jonic, he doesn't know," said the blue goblin. He looked at Drew. "Lukais has her."

Drew cursed. "Did you lead her into a trap?" he demanded.

Hair instantly bristled outward like porcupine quills all over their bodies and they both moved toward him threateningly. Drew backed up and put out his hands. "Sorry -- sorry. I'm really worried about her and this whole faerie thing has me off balance. You've got to admit you guys don't have the greatest reputation where I come from." They both grinned widely and the quills disappeared. "How did you get in here anyway?" he asked. "Nobody said anything about goblins gaining access to this place."

"Everything's off balance," said Jonic. "It was

quite easy. We were told where to find you."

Drew hid his surprise. "Irfin?"

Jonic nodded.

"Umm, well I thought leprechauns and goblins --
"

Sirt put a finger up to his lips. "You must swear not to tell. Our reputation is very important."

"Okay." That would be easy, Drew thought. He didn't anticipate talking to other goblins. "How do I get to Pandimora?"

"You can't," said Sirt.

"Listen, I've been through this with Irfin --" he shut up as they began to look hostile again. Drew took a deep breath. "Last time I saw goblins, they were screaming to get their hands on a human."

Both goblins smirked.

"That's true." Jonic nodded vigorously, his large ears flopping. "But that was business. This is more personal. We like Pandimora," he added. "She's got guts going up against the elder. She asked us to get her into Aisywel but the elder caught us and he suspended her in a dimension without time or meaning."

"Wait -- he caught all of you? How did you escape?"

"Listen," Jonic turned surly. "We didn't have to come for you. Pandimora begged the elder to release us, which is lucky for all of us, okay? Now here's the plan. We might be able to shift you into the dimension, but it's very risky."

"Tell me what to do."

"We disassemble your cells and body matter bit by bit and piece by piece and then when you reach the other side, the cells and body matter come back together."

"Seriously? What if you miss putting a few cells back in their proper place -- like brain cells or something?"

They just looked at him.

Drew rubbed the back of his neck, picturing Pandimora alone ... a prisoner. "And then what? How do we get out again?"

"Once we get you to Pandimora, you have to initiate the shift for both of you to Aisywel and then to Isidghe almost instantly. Pandimora entered Aisywel from Isidghe and must go back in the same order so her equilibrium is not left unbalanced." Sirt looked at Jonic. "Right? Isn't that the way we have to do it?"

Jonic shrugged his narrow shoulders. "Maybe."

Drew looked at them. "You're not sure?"

"What we do know is there can be no delay; the shift must be almost instantaneous."

"What happens if it doesn't work that way?" Drew asked grimly. "What if something prevents us from shifting quickly?"

"Hmm, well," Sirt hedged, "we don't really know."

"There's no other option?" Drew asked, frustrated. "That's a lot of cell and body shifting," he muttered.

Sirt waved his hand. "Oh, don't worry," he said, "We do this all the time and we're perfectly fine."

Drew looked at his misshapen face, frighteningly wide grin and bulging purple eyes. "Thanks for the reassurance," he managed. If he wanted to find

Pandimora, he saw no other option.

***

Drew's body shook as all his cells came back together. He looked down at his palms, watched them solidify into skin and bone and muscle. He stood in a place with no clearly defined matter at all. The surface upon which he stood seemed to have no clear definition and he wasn't certain if it was even solid under his feet. Everything around him was a vast white space.

"Pandimora," he whispered as the goblins had instructed.

Instantly, she was beside him, her arms coming around him tightly as if she would never let him go. "Drew! By all the faeries, you are alive and well." She placed kisses on his mouth and he put his arms around her, but then she pushed him away from her, her eyes sparking in anger. "Why are you here?" Her voice was almost a screech and he covered his ears.

She reached for him again. "I'm sorry."

"Sirt and Jonic." He hadn't been sure any of this was true or that it would work. He touched her forehead, pushed the curling red hair back from her face. Her eyes were red and he was angry that Lukais had made this sweet faerie cry. But there was no time for delay.

"We have to get out of here now." He opened his palm to reveal ancient silver coins the goblins had given him. "One for you and one for me. Concentrate on returning to Aisywel, just as if you were opening a portal," he said. Even as the words left his mouth they both began the transition into transparency and dissolved from the white space.

They materialized in a place that reminded Drew of the healing sanctuary. He had only a moment to scan its breathtaking beauty and the large glass enclosed building beside them before he saw the two goblins running toward them. The air swirled with strange dark currents that made him uneasy.

"Quickly." Sirt and Jonic reached them but Pandimora darted away.

In disbelief, Drew watched her run to the front of the tall glass building. "Pandimora!"

She looked over her shoulder. "I must meet the elder council as I should have done that first day." Her legs moved incredibly fast and she disappeared into the building. He looked back at the goblins then ran after her.

"It may be too late," called Jonic after him. "Um, and Lukais implied he would kill us last time we were here, if we came back."

Drew turned his head as he reached the corner of the building. "Get out now."

Sirt nodded. "Hurry. With each passing heartbeat the peril increases."

"Thank you," Drew said and ran into the building, skidding to a stop inside the doorway. Pandimora stood in the middle of an enormous open room, opulently furnished with glowing tables and chairs of glass, the floor some type of shattered glass that had been reconstructed. On her knees, she struggled to rise.

Drew ran to her and pulled her to her feet. He saw the mark on her arm glowing bright red.

"The human."

Drew recognized the same deep, ominous voice

he'd heard before in his office. His adrenalin raced, heart pumping fast. A regal older man in white robes with shoulder-length white hair sat at a glass table facing them. His ice-blue eyes assessed them without emotion.

Drew quickly looked for a means of escape but the room was circular, and even the door he'd entered appeared gone.

"I am frankly amazed at your tenacity, Pandimora," said the elder. "If you seek the high elder council, they have wisely moved their meeting with the insurgents to the southern hemisphere."

Drew felt the tension radiating through Pandimora. He reached for her hand and pulled it behind him, palming her a silver goblin coin. She took it but in the next instant Drew saw two coins appear on the glass table in front of the elder.

Lukais picked up the coins and casually tossed them in the air. They burst into blue flames and disintegrated.

Pandimora squeezed his hand and he felt her shaking. He remembered the crystal expert warning against making a faerie mad. Looking at the fury in the elder's eyes, he knew then it was very, very bad.

***

The elven star vibrated on Pandimora's arm. At first the sensation puzzled her, but then with each passing moment she grew stronger and more clearheaded. She controlled her mounting excitement. In her mind she manifested a ground portal under herself and Drew. She didn't dare look at him but hoped he dropped down into the portal and escaped.

He fell into the hole, still holding her hand, but Lukais dashed her attempt at escape and her hand was pulled from Drew's.

"No!" Drew tried to hold onto her but he was sucked into the portal. Lukais effortlessly levitated her to his table.

"The human doesn't concern me. But you Pandimora have wanted to return so now you will stay." The elder steepled his fingers and leaned his chin upon them, studying her. "Your mother also was very clever. She learned to communicate with the faeries as a child. I was the one who invited her to our beautiful and magnificent realm." His eyes held a faraway look. "We became good friends."

Pandimora hardly dared to move, part of her thirsty to hear of her mother. He speared her with his blue gaze. "Only I could soothe the headaches she suffered. We formed a bond, but when she met my good friend Declan, they had eyes only for each other." He said it quite dispassionately, but she wondered if Lukais had also loved Clare. "The high lord of the faeries and a human."

"Where are they?" She clenched her fists. Ever since she had found out about her parents, a burning desire had gripped her to know the truth. Where could she find them? Was Irfin correct, they were burned into the afterlife?

He waved a hand. "Gone."

Pain ripped through her, but she put her shoulders back. "I wonder after all this time that I never sensed the cruelty that is your nature. What a pretense, the high elder who cared about all worlds and dimensions, but all you really cared about was the power and your own sense of importance. What you plan is wrong, Lukais."

"It's progress, Pandimora. I do care about both you and Lilja. I spent so much time mentoring you two, thinking to mold Lilja as a future elder." His brows drew together sternly. "You returned to Aisywel to protect your sister, when in effect she too has defected to the humans. And she too will have to answer for abandoning her birthright." His words shattered the short-lived relief Pandimora had felt on hearing that her sister was safe.

Refusing to be treated like a pawn, Pandimora moved right up against the council table. He watched her through narrowed eyes. "You have become quite bold. I always knew of the rebellion you kept in check, but you never voiced it."

"I've grown up," she said, gripping the edge of the glass with her fingers. "The council will be told what you have done and they will decide your fate. Our world is changing and you will have no option but to change with it. The Aisywel crystals have been witness to all that has occurred," she added. "You will be judged upon your words and actions."

Lukais now towered over her. "Surely you don't think I will just go away, Pandimora? That would be naive of you."

"There may be no choice."

Lukais grabbed her arm and pulled her over the table toward him. "What you will never understand is the grave responsibility I bear. Difficult decisions must be made."

It was eerily similar to what Irtin had said.

Her elven star radiated, allowing her the

strength to jerk her arm free. She shoved the table toward Lukais but he jumped into the air and avoided its impact.

White bolts of light struck the glass floor all around her. She gripped Irfin's device in her pants pocket, having forgotten she still had it from when she'd brought Drew to the sanctuary. But the device seemed to yield her nothing so she dove around the upturned table and avoided more flashes of light. She knew if they hit her she would suffer the same burns as before, except this time he would make sure she died.

The glass floor partially shattered, falling down into the ground beneath her, leaving gaping holes in the floor structure. Moving swiftly, she avoided the elder's grasp and ran toward the still-glowing portal, but her foot slipped into one of the gaping holes and she lost her balance.

The glass edge of the hole scraped along her leg and ankle, cutting into her skin. She pulled herself away from the hole but Lukais pulled her up and flung her through the air and across the room. She landed hard on a solid section of flooring, sliding across the glass, then rolled, putting out her arms to stop her momentum.

Knowing she couldn't remain still, she scrambled to her feet, gripping her elven star with one hand, willing the strength and protection of the star to fully activate. She ignored the pain in her ankle and leg, and reaching into her pocket, she again gripped the device. The elder ran toward her, a great winged creature in white, his blue eyes mesmerizing even from this distance. She had no defense and in disgust she threw Irfin's device, hearing it bounce against the wall and then roll along the floor.

She retreated to the wall, assessing her chances for escape. The elder was almost upon her when he suddenly stepped on Irfin's discarded device and his feet went out from under him.

Seizing her opportunity, she jumped past him and lifting her arm in a sweeping gesture she expanded her still activated portal upwards, but the elder caught her arm just as Drew ran through the portal. With a mighty heave Drew tossed her the sword he held. In one fluid move Pandimora turned and plunged the glistening bronze sword deep into the elder's white robes.

Luminescent green light shot out of the elder's back, shards flying like glass, shattering the ceiling, raining glass down on their heads. Pandimora struggled to hold onto the sword as the force of their connection vibrated her arms and hands. She pulled the blade out and green light shot out the front of Lukais' robes, likewise imploding the glass walls. Pandimora pulled Drew backwards. "Don't let the light touch you," she cried.

As the elder staggered, the green light hit the glass as he twisted and turned. Pandimora grabbed Drew's hand and they dropped into the portal, falling to the wood floor of his office.

As they lay there on the floor in his office, she opened her fingers and the sword clattered to the wood floor.

They both stared at the sword which now lay beside them. "Close the portal," he said, breathing hard.

Pandimora waved her hands and it dissolved.

"That was too close." Drew looked at the sword. "There's something about this sword. After the first attack, Irfin said he would attach a device to the hilt." He touched the small disc wedged between the double swirled handle. "Will the elder come after us?" he asked.

"Not right away," she said. Drew put the sword on the table and Pandimora stared in fascination at the blood stains. The blade was no longer a magnificent bronze color but now a dull green with chips along its edges.

"In the earth dimension this sword truly looks its age," she said. "But in the faerie world, it reverted back to its ancient origins." She looked up, her eyes filled with moisture. "I was so worried about you, Drew, when I had to leave you."

"You saved my life." He pressed a kiss to the top of her head. Pandimora stood on tiptoe and kissed him back.

Drew sat down in his desk chair with her on his lap. "I never wanted to fall in love again, Pandimora. I can't bear the thought of letting you go."

Pandimora put her arms around his neck and leaned her head against him. "I love you, Drew. There's so much we have to figure out," she said. "Unanswered questions. But I hope at least the elder has been stopped and Aisywel is safe."

***

Drew knocked on the ornately carved door and it swung open immediately.

"Good evening, Mr. Maddox," said the butler.

"Hi, Branson. I just wanted to stop by and offer

my condolences on Mary's passing."

Branson nodded. "The family is gathered in the kitchen, if you'd like to come inside."

"I don't want to intrude. I didn't know her that well but ..." his voice trailed away as Irfin appeared in the hallway. He looked like the picture Mary had given Drew, a gray-haired, eighty-year-old man.

"That's okay, Branson, I'll talk with Drew," said the little man.

Branson nodded and then Irfin walked across the Italian marble floor, indicating they should go into a room to the right. Drew had first met with Mary in this very room. Irfin closed the door and Drew took a seat on the same blue brocade chair while Irfin sat at the desk.

"I'm sure you're surprised to see me like this," Irfin said.

"Not really. Remember, I had the pictures Mary gave me."

"This is the face I present in the human world. As you first saw me in the magical dimension, that is my immortal face."

"So you put on a facade for each world?"

Irfin frowned, then said slowly. "Yes, I guess that is how it is."

"And are you really a sorcerer?"

"In one of my lives yes. In this life, I'm a retired inventor."

"I stopped in to say I'm sorry on Mary's passing," Drew said. "I won't stay but a minute. I wanted to return the check your wife gave me as a down payment."

Irfin looked surprised. "She told me about your

meetings." Irfin shrugged, playing with a glass paperweight. "It's yours. You certainly earned it."

"Not really. I didn't finish the job. And we both know the rest of the story."

Irfin looked very subdued. "I kept thinking about what you said. All Mary wanted was to have me here with her. I've given it up, you know," Irfin added quietly. "Mary was my eighteenth wife. I've outlived every one of them. My children, my grandchildren. I'm not going back."

"So you've walked away from all of it?"

"Yes. And you were right, Drew. Lukais promised an immortal life for Mary if I could secure the crystal. It wasn't what Mary wanted and certainly not at the expense of others. She just wanted me to be with her and the kids for however long we had. And now that she's gone, I'm going to do the human thing and be mortal like everyone else. I'm sorry for the harm I caused you and Pandimora. Aisywel is moving toward complete chaos. I don't know how it will ever recover. Lukais will fight the netherworld invasion possibly at great loss of life. I fear it will lead to a bitter end for our world."

"Well," Drew said, "we had a confrontation with him and Pandimora may have killed him. She plunged my Celtic sword into him and he appeared to split apart."

"I wish I could believe it would be so simple, but he is incredibly powerful and not easily disposed of. I guess Pandimora was right. I shouldn't have doubted her." He looked at Drew. "And what about you, Drew? I am glad you decided to set aside your fears."

"I don't know what you mean."

Irfin smiled. "Living life each day without fear of the past repeating itself. If what the elder said was true, and I'm not saying it is that Pandimora inherited her mother's condition, are you willing to take that leap of faith and love her anyway?"

"I love her and quite honestly I think the elder was wrong. Either way, we're taking it a day at a time, figuring out how it can all work." Drew sighed, standing. "Pandimora promised not to return to Aisywel until we know for sure if he's gone."

Irfin accompanied him to the door. "We managed to wind back time, you know, before Mary died. We had an additional two days."

Drew stared at Irfin who suddenly seemed very old.

"Wait." Irfin opened a drawer in an ornately carved table beside the door. He pulled out something wrapped in a black jeweler's cloth. Even before Drew took it, he could feel the shift of the air around them.

Accepting the wrapped cloth, Drew felt the two crystals inside.

Irfin nodded. "The crystals. I hope in time she will return them to their proper place. There will be a long struggle, I'm afraid." Irfin turned and walked away.

Placing the envelope with the check on the small table beside the door, Drew let himself out. He put the crystals into his jacket pocket, feeling their vibrations radiating through the cloth.

Drew pulled his jacket collar up around his neck as the snow and wind swirled around him. He looked up at the sky. The weather forecast had been for sunshine, but the sky looked black and threatening. He wondered about Aisywel and the chaos both Irfin and Pandimora predicted. He supposed the weather would get much, much worse in the coming days and perhaps weeks ahead.

When he opened the door to his truck, Drew was surprised to see a large manila envelope on the seat. Curious, he picked it up.

There was no stamp but the return address of an accounting firm immediately caught his eye. Deborah's debt. How had it gotten into his truck? Had they finally decided to sue him for the money? He carefully slit open the envelope. Inside was an executed one-page release. The balance had been paid in full.

Drew looked up at Irfin's house. Had it been Mary -- or had it been Irfin? He refolded the sheet and carefully placed it in his back pocket.

∞ Epilogue ∞

Pandimora walked toward Drew's home as the snow fell gently all around her. Still very much in tune with her homeland, she felt its chaos through every part of her body. She had not returned to her dear Aisywel nor had Lukais tried to follow them, if he was still alive.

The faerie realm faced a bleak future unless a fearless leader could unite the worlds. Her homeland was breaking apart, her family was still missing. As of now, she had decided not to activate a portal until she had formed a solid plan of action. Aisywel had become too dangerous and unstable. Now she had to find Lilja, if indeed she was on the earth realm.

Drew was at his brother Grey's ranch on the outskirts of town since the weather had hampered his efforts until today. Amazingly, Drew's home appeared untouched from the explosion. Pandimora wondered if Irfin had somehow thrown the explosion into another dimension. As for fulfilling her bargain with the goblins, Drew had promised to see what he could do for the next Halloween celebration in town. But it would be a celebration for adults only. He didn't want to take a chance on children inadvertently coming into contact with the goblins.

Pandimora reached the front of the house as Drew's truck pulled into the driveway. She met him halfway and they shared a lingering kiss. "You'll freeze with no coat," he chided, pulling an extra heavy coat from his truck and helping her button into it.

"Faeries don't feel the cold," she reminded him, but she snuggled into the coat and inhaled his scent.

"There's something in the pocket for you," he said.

Looking at him, she pulled out the rolled up black cloth. Her breath caught with excitement as she saw the crystals inside. "Where did you get them?" she asked in soft amazement.

"Irfin. From what I can figure out, he cut all ties with Lukais. I imagine he's kept them protected and hidden in some way. He wanted you to have them."

"Oh my, oh my." She pressed them to her chest.

"Pandimora, I thought about this on the way home. Is there a way to ask the crystals about your family?"

She nodded, and still holding the crystals to her chest, she closed her eyes a moment. A hologram appeared as they stood there. Pandimora, her brother, baby sister and her parents sat eating at a large wooden table. Laughter and conversation flowed, their caring for each other evident. Clare stood and walked around to each of them, one arm cradling the infant, gently touching each of them on their shoulder and kissing the top of Pandimora and Kirklas' heads. She leaned against her husband. Declan, hair dark and eyes a sparkling green put his arm around her waist. Clare looked so different from the other hologram. Love and calm assurance shone in her eyes for those gathered.

Drew saw the tears in Pandimora's eyes. "I didn't

think Irfin could make up for all he did wrong, but seeing the look in your eyes now, I was wrong," he said. "He's given you an unbelievable gift."

Without words she wrapped the crystals and put them almost reverently back into the jacket pocket.

"Thank you." She finally said, softly. "I was always fascinated with human life. I visited upon occasion, but never did I envision I would come to love a human so profoundly." Her kiss stirred the embers of the fire never burning far from the surface in Drew.

He held her in his arms as the snow fell on them.

"Were you able to see your brother?" she asked.

Drew nodded. "Yeah, it was odd though. I'm sure I saw a woman but then she disappeared. My brother Grey didn't want to talk about it and I could see he was torn up about something. He did mention a woman's name. Lilja. Kind of unusual --"

Pandimora gave a high-pitched scream. "My sister!"

Grey tensed. "Lilja -- you never said her name! There could be only one, right? We need to go to my brother's ranch. Your sister was there."

Pandimora put a hand to her heart as joy raced through her.

They walked swiftly to his truck. Pandimora was so excited her trembling fingers had trouble opening the door. Drew reached past her and pulled it open, helping her into the vehicle.

They reversed out of the driveway and into the road. Pandimora squeezed her hands tightly. Lilja was found!

Now she had to find Kirklas.

∞ *THE END* ∞

Once and Always

Memory could be gentle. At other times it left scars.

Anna Barlow had read those words this morning and somehow they felt like a reflection of her life. She stared out over her ranch's fields now, trying to shake off the cobwebs of old memories...

She had to live with her mistakes, but somehow she'd find a way out of this mess.

Heartstealer

Jacie's stomach churned as she stared at the ground two thousand feet below. What insanity made her put herself through this punishment—just to prove she wasn't washed up as a stunt woman?

"Just do it," she muttered. "You've done it thousands of times before. Get your foot out the door and jump."

Echoes From the Past

A woman, a man and a child with nothing in common but their respective troubled pasts. Three wounded souls determined to survive alone until they realize all they need to heal is each other.

On the verge of a nervous breakdown, Christie reacts by running away, emotionally and physically. Down to her last twenty dollars, she's determined to fulfill her dead sister's last wish -- to locate their sister Judith who left home twenty years before. Her quest brings her into the lives of Garrett, Judith's husband, and the emotionally fragile Hannah, Judith's daughter.

Soulmates Through Time: Book 2 Time travel series. Thrust from her own time in 1822, Elise has been separated from the man she loves for 24 years. She has adjusted to modern times, raised a daughter, and become successful in her own right. When she stumbles upon the way back, she must make the decision to step back into that time.

Will Darien still love her and will Elise be able to turn back the clock and regain the love they once shared? Does she want to turn back time?

Treasure So Rare: Book 3 Time Travel series. Captain Erik Remington has been haunted for three years by a black haired sea witch. They spent seven glorious days and nights before she vanished as mysteriously as she appeared.

In 1850, when his ship is pulled into a strange vortex, he ends up in middle ages England.

¤ ¤ ¤

Romantic Short Stories

Two Babies, a Cowboy and Sara: Short, sweet romance, 24,000 words. When Sara is appointed co-guardian of her deceased cousin's infant girls, their father Lucas is glad to accept Sara's help in caring for the twins. For Sara it's a labor of love and also a dream come true since she can't have babies of her own.

For Lucas, having Sara on his ranch is a reminder of how his life could have turned out so very differently, if only he'd met Sara first.

Deception

Short, sweet romance with a hint of suspense. Trey's boss is old, sick and his days are numbered;

and he wants to see his missing granddaughter Katharine before he dies. Trey will do almost anything for the old man, even if it means having artist Sacha Fortune pretend to be Katharine.

But Sacha has more to lose than Trey could ever guess.

Faeries Lost Series

Find Me ~ Book 1: Pandimora loves the faerie realm Aisywel, but she's a bit of a rebel, has little interest in the rich faerie history, loves to listen in on private conversations and hops portals into the earth realm against the advice of the high elders.

All in all her independent spirit isn't going so well in the faerie realm, but what she knows about herself as a faerie will be sorely tested when she is kicked out of Aisywel and forced to confront a terrible crime by one of her own high elders.

Whisper Me ~ Book 2: Greyson Maddox's horses are inexplicably falling ill. He begins to hear a woman's voice singing a haunting Celtic song during the night. The only thing is, he's in the middle of a snow storm in a pretty isolated area. Where is that voice coming from, and who is singing to his horses?

Lilja appears out of nowhere, literally -- claiming to be a faerie. Her appearance, combined with his horses gradually recovering their health, will challenge everything Greyson knows about life...or thought he knew.

Hear Me ~ Book 3: Heir to high lord of the

faeries, Kirklas has managed to escape the living hell he's been exiled to for the last 10 human years. Upon his return home to Aisywel, everything is changed. Beset with civil unrest, Aisywel is in turmoil and everyone he loved is gone, and with them any hope for answers. Can he set aside the thirst for revenge or will he follow that road to its bitter end? A road that may well destroy him and the life he once hoped for.

Visit my author page at www.GraceBrannigan.com to read all my contemporary, time travel, faerie stories and short romantic stories.

Grace Brannigan

www.ingramcontent.com/pod-product-compliance
Lightning Source LLC
Chambersburg PA
CBHW071504170626
46811CB00007B/2733